12 FAVOURITE
BIBLE STORIES

By
Sheila Daw

Copyright © Sheila Daw 2017
This book is sold subject to the condition that it shall not, by way of trade or otherwise, be lent, resold, hired out, or otherwise circulated without the publisher's prior consent in any form of binding or cover other than that in which it is published and without a similar condition including this condition being imposed on the subsequent publisher.
The moral right of Sheila Daw has been asserted.
ISBN-13: 978-1545478844
ISBN-10: 1545478848

This book is dedicated to all my readers. As they read this book, I pray they will love and enjoy these amazing stories as they come alive.

CONTENTS

1. Joseph The Dreamer 1
2. Moses 23
3. David The Shepherd King 35
4. Ruth 46
5. Queen Esther 56
6. Daniel 67
7. The Miracle Jar Of Oil 76
8. Martha & Mary 84
9. Jairus's Little Daughter 92
10. Zacchaeus The Tax Collector & Blind Bartimaeus 97
11. A Small Boy's Lunch 102
12. The Nativity 114

1

JOSEPH THE DREAMER

My Early Years

My father Jacob lived in the land of Canaan with my mother Rachel, his second wife Leah, their maidservants and my 10 brothers. My father was a prosperous land and livestock owner. The God of my great grandfather Abraham & my grandfather Isaac has blessed him in every imaginable way.

We live in tents made of animal skins and regularly have to pack up our home and move around the country. Father had a lot of livestock cattle, donkeys, sheep, goats and camels, so in order to give the animals the best grazing we had to constantly move our home.

I remember the time, when I was very young we were on the move again, and I was walking along the road with my mother. I over-heard my father talking to my mother, saying that he was going to meet up with my Uncle Esau for the first time for many years.

He was worried about the meeting, as there had been a big family argument and he hadn't seen or spoken to his brother since that time. Apparently the disagreement had been so bad between my father and uncle, that he wanted to kill my father and so he had to flee for his life.

We were walking along the road very slowly all of a sudden, in the distance my father saw Uncle Esau walking towards him! I remember we all stopped and everyone went very quiet! My uncle also stopped and then amazingly started running towards my father and it was a wonderful reunion. They were so pleased to see each other and hugged each other for a long time. God had performed a miracle and now there was no more hate and anger.

Benjamin and I are my father's two youngest sons, and we are very special to him. We were born to our mother who was the love of his life. Sadly during the birth of my brother Benjamin, my mother died which was a great sadness to my father.

I remember it was very hard when my mother died, as I was young, and I couldn't understand why she was no longer with us and I missed her very much. It was especially difficult for Benjamin as he was brought up by a nurse, and never knew his mother. I found it hard to think she would never see us grow up.

My father never got over losing my mother, as he loved her very much.

Benjamin and I were very close and we would play together for hours. As we grew older we would go off for the day and look after father's sheep.

I loved my father very much and had a special relationship with him, more so than any of my other brothers. I knew that I was the favourite, as I was born after many years of my parents believing and trusting God to give them a child, and then a couple of years later Benjamin was born.

One day my father gave me a special gift! It was the most beautiful coat which was made up of a unique design in vibrant colours and had gold thread running through it. It was a rich beautifully woven coat. The robe had long sleeves and was full length down to the ground. It was not really suitable for every day work but more for special occasions.

When my father gave me this coat, it caused a lot of jealously and resentment, amongst my brothers as they were never given anything special, and everyone knew that I was the favourite. At times I found it difficult as my brothers gave me a hard time and weren't very kind to me.

My brothers began to hate me because I was the favourite and loved by our father. Sometimes, when I looked at them I could feel they hated me. They could not say a kind word to me and would tease and laugh at me.

I was a good looking, strong young man at 17 years old! Everybody kept telling me this! I must admit I did enjoy the flattery. I would often dream about the future. Marry a beautiful girl, have a family and become a wealthy livestock and landowner like my father.

One night, I had two dreams, which I decided to share with my brothers and father. I didn't understand them and wondered what they meant. Sharing these dreams made my brothers even more resentful of me.

The first dream I had, I saw that my sheaf of corn stood up right and taller than my brothers and their sheaves of corn were bowing down to mine.

My second dream was similar to the first, the sun, moon and eleven stars were bowing down to me.

My brothers were furious with me and my father was not too pleased either, they teased and mocked me calling me dreamer boy. They told me I lived in my own world of make believe. Who did I think I was?! I was only the youngest of my family! No one would ever listen to me and I would never amount to anything in life!

As I thought about it, I was probably unwise to share these dreams with them and I came over rather full of myself! I was young and excited but needed to learn when to share the things that are given to me by God. I was longing to understand what they meant and wanted to discuss their meanings.

I knew my brothers were whispering behind my back, they would stop talking when I came near them, and call out to me in their mocking tones. I was sure that they would love to kill me one day. They all ganged up on my except for Benjamin who was still young and didn't understand what it was all about.

It made me feel lonely and left out, and I found it hard to ignore them. However, despite this, I knew God had a specific plan and destiny for my life but had no idea how this would unfold.

My brothers were nomadic shepherds, and they decided one day, to take their flocks of sheep and goats to fresh grazing which was much further away from our home.

They had been away for several weeks, and my father wanted to make sure that they were alright and send some food provisions to them. I was asked to go and take food to my brothers. I loaded up the donkey with all the provisions and set off. It was a journey which took several days. When I got to the place where they were meant to be I was told, by another shepherd, that they had moved on to another area, so I travelled on until I found them.

Pit To Palace

I was young and naïve and hoped I could win my brothers over. When I arrived tired after several days journeying, they were brusque with me. They had obviously already seen me coming and were talking about me. They had a hard cruel look in their eyes, although, my eldest brother Reuben was a little kinder to me than the rest of them.

I arrived and got off my donkey, unpacked the provisions, and without any warning they pushed and shoved me and then grabbed me. They ripped off my beautiful ornate robe threw it on to the ground and dragged me to the edge of a deep dark water cistern! I cried out and pleaded with them, hoping that one of my brothers would stop the others! They held me over the gapping dark hole and then pushed me over.

I remember the horror, as I went hurtling down, down into the dark deep water cistern at great speed and landed with a thud at the bottom. Fortunately, it wasn't filled with water! My head was spinning and I sat there very bruised, shaken and shocked! As I looked up, it seemed miles away, I saw a little shaft of light and could see and hear one of my brothers rolling a heavy lid over the top of the hole. I sat there in total darkness very scared.

JOSEPH THE DREAMER

I began to wonder what would happen to me, are they going to leave me there to starve to death. I was hungry, scared and bruised.

I guessed they were sitting down to discuss what a good job they had just done! They were happy that I was now out of the way – or so they thought!

I also imagined them enjoying the food that I had just brought them! Their hearts had become so hard and full of evil that they didn't care anymore. The main thing on their minds was to get rid of me!

After some considerable time, one of my brothers, Simeon rolled the lid off the water cistern and threw a rope down to me and pulled me up. I was surprised, but as I came up out of the cistern, I saw a large train of camels coming over the desert. The camels were loaded down with all sorts of spices and silks as they were on their way to Egypt.

Judah, my second eldest brother, called out to the men, who were from a place called Midian. They stopped them and went over to talk to them. There was a lot of arguing, raised voices and arm waving. I guess they were haggling over a price! They generously decided it would be better to sell me as a slave rather than to kill me, because I was after all still their brother, and their own flesh and blood! It would be a good way of getting rid of me forever without harming me!

My brothers talked to the men, agreed on a price and sold me for 20 shekels (which was the local currency). They handed me over to them and then one by one they walked away without turning around. I saw two of my brother, Dan and Naphtali rubbing their hands with glee – their mission had been accomplished!

I walked alongside the camel train, with my head hanging down pondering my future, as the camel train started lumbering off across the desert. I didn't know if I would be well treated, or if I would even arrive in Egypt, they might try and get rid of me too along the way!

Although, I was totally alone and confused, I began to think about the stories, my father told us, about the way God protected and looked after him in many difficult situations. I remembered, about the time my Uncle Esau who was very angry with my father, over a big family disagreement, how years later there had been a wonderful reconciliation between them.

I was in a very difficult and horrible situation, but I knew that God was still with me and was not going to leave me alone. Although my brothers hated me, and were against me, and only wanted bad things to happen to me, God was going to turn things around for my good because he had a plan and purpose for my life.

I heard many years later, that to cover up for what they had done to me, they decided to kill a goat and put my beautiful woven coat into the blood, making out that I had been killed by a wild animal. After all, what would they say to my father when they returned home as I hadn't come back with them.

I can't imagine what my father went through when he got the news! He had not only lost his wife now his favourite son!

JOSEPH THE DREAMER

After weeks of travelling across the desert in the scorching heat, the camel train finally arrived in Egypt. The Midianites didn't know what to do with me, as they didn't really want me either and they had made that very clear! After much discussion and negotiating, no doubt for a good price, they sold me again to one of Pharaoh's officials called Potiphar.

I was now in a foreign country and amongst foreigners. I couldn't speak the language and still didn't know what was going to happen to me! I had no family, friends or anything familiar around me, but I knew deep down God was still with me. I can't explain it but He was there. However, I longed with all my heart to be back in our tents with my father. I could picture him as the sun was setting, sitting at the entrance of his tent in the cool of the day.

I was taken to live in the house of my new master Potiphar. As time went by, Potiphar noticed that everything I did had a standard of excellence about it. I stood out above all the other staff in Potiphar's Palace. God began to bless me in whatever I did.

One day, Potiphar called me into his office, and told me that he was going to promote me, and put me in charge of his household in the Palace and everything he owned. I had a large number of staff under my control. Everything prospered under my care. He had complete trust and confidence in me. I was reliable and faithful in everything I did, and showed integrity in whatever I was asked to do.

Potiphar travelled and was often away from home for several weeks at a time, leaving me in charge of all the daily affairs of the Palace and his personal life.

One day, I was going about my duties as I normally did, and because my master Potiphar was away again I had extra responsibilities.

Potiphar's wife over the last few weeks, constantly wanted to talk to me and stop me from doing my work. I became very uncomfortable in her company but she kept trying to get me to stay and spend time with her.

One day, while her husband was still away, she tried to make me do things that were wrong. I told her that the things she wanted me to do were wrong, and I would not do it, as my Master trusted me and had given me a lot of responsibility. I decided to avoid her and keep out of her way. I sent one of my other staff to attend to her.

Potiphar's wife became very angry with me and decided to make up lies about me. When Potiphar returned home, she accused me of things that I had never done. Everything she said about me was false and untrue.

Palace To Prison

Owing to all the lies and accusations my master Potiphar became very angry with me. I was unable to talk to him, which made it impossible for me to be able to defend myself. As a result I lost my job and was thrown into prison for many years!

Life seemed to be going from bad to worse! I was in prison for a very long time! What was this all about? Yet again, there were more misunderstandings and lies!

There seemed to be so much injustice and I was unable to explain my situation to anyone. What had happened to my dreams of the future? What did those dreams mean when I was 17 years old? When is all this hardness going to end?

During this time, I had to make a decision not to allow bitterness and resentment take a hold of me, as I knew it would make things even worse. I called out to the God of my forefathers Abraham and Isaac to help me and be with me.

Unbeknown to me, the prison warden began to notice that I was different from all the other prisoners. The prison warden started giving me responsibilities in the prison above the other prisoners. He began to trust me and put me in charge when he was not around. I knew it was God giving me favour. Despite all the hard and difficult times, I knew that God's favour was on me and He was looking after me.

I was going about my duties one particular day, and the prison warden, called me aside, to say that two of Pharaoh's officials were being thrown into prison as they had fallen out of favour with Pharaoh! I was being assigned to look after them.

They were the chief butler and baker. Both these officials, especially the butler were people of high rank and importance. Owing to the confidential nature of their employment, as well as their access to the King, they were generally the highest nobles or had royal connections.

The butler had a very important position. He was not only the butler but also the cup-bearer to the King. He looked after the royal vineyards, and the cellars where they kept the vats of wine. He also probably had a lot of staff under him.

The Cupbearer had to do everything in the king's presence - the cup was washed, the juice of the grapes pressed into it and it was then handed to the King.

The baker or cook had an equally important job. He had to look after everything relating to the providing and preparing of meals for the royal table.

Whilst they were in prison, the butler and the baker each had a dream and they didn't know what the dream meant. I noticed they were very sad and discouraged one day, so I asked them what was wrong. They told me that they had each had a dream. God had given me the ability to interpret dreams. So I asked them to tell me their dreams.

The chief cupbearer then proceeded to tell me his dream. "He saw a vine in front of him and on the vine were three branches. As soon as it budded, it blossomed, and the clusters ripened into grapes. Pharaoh's cup was in my hand, and I took the grapes, squeezed them into Pharaoh's cup and put the cup in his hand."

I told him the meaning. The three branches are three days. Within three days Pharaoh will restore you to your position and you will put Pharaoh's cup into his hand, just as you used to do when you were his cupbearer.

The butler was very relieved and happy as you can imagine!

I asked him when all goes well with you, remember me and show me kindness; please mention me to Pharaoh and get me out of this prison. I explained how I was forcibly carried off from the land of Canaan, and even here I have done nothing to deserve being put in a prison.

Although I was trusting God, I was longing with all my heart to get out of this prison! I guessed that the purpose of my being in the prison was all part of the preparation for my destiny- whatever that may be!

The chief baker then told me his dream. "He said on my head were three baskets of bread. In the top basket were all kinds of baked goods for Pharaoh, but the birds were eating them out of the basket on my head."

I again explained his dream. The three baskets are three days. Within three days Pharaoh will lift off your head and hang your body up on a pole. And the birds will eat away your flesh.

A day or so later, it was Pharaoh's birthday, and he was giving a feast for all his officials.

Pharaoh is the most important and powerful person in the kingdom. He is the head of the government and high priest of every temple. The people of Egypt considered the Pharaoh to be a half-man, half-god. The Pharaoh owned all of Egypt.

Exactly, as I told the officials would happen to them happened! Pharaoh restored the chief cupbearer to his position, so that he once again put the cup into Pharaoh's hand. The chief baker was executed, just as I had said to them in the interpretations.

The chief cupbearer, however, did not remember me! Once he was back in the Palace, he was busy with all his duties and everything was going well for him. He forgot all about me!

I was left in prison for another two years. I often felt forgotten by Pharaoh, the world and at times God. However, I continued to trust God to work out His plans and purposes. The drudgery of my life and job day in and day out continued, I didn't have a day's break from prison life! I often wondered if it would ever come to an end or if this was going to be my lot!

I had feelings of loneliness and despair, after all I was human, but I was willing to trust God, and believed that He would work things out.

I had a lot of time in prison to think. I had to make many choices! I chose to believe God was using every single thing that had happened in my life. All the misunderstandings; rejection by my brothers; being thrown down a pit; arriving in Egypt with no family or friends; promoted to the Palace; then being falsely accused by Potiphar's wife; thrown into prison and then the final straw being forgotten by the King's cupbearer whose dream I had interpreted! The cupbearer was now fulfilling his destiny! What about my destiny?

What had happened to the dreams I was given when I was a young man of 17 years old with so much hope and promise ahead of me – and now to this! My dreams and destiny were apparently on hold!

Thirteen years since first receiving my dreams had passed! It appeared that life was passing me by! Little did I know that God was about to turn my life upside down but I had to keep trusting Him.

Then one day, I woke up as usual, following the same routine for another day of fulfilling the same duties.

Somehow, that morning felt different, I had a sense that this was not going to be just "another" day.

I was on my usual rounds, when suddenly, one of the servants came running down into the prison and shouted, "Joseph! Joseph! You have been summoned to come up to the Palace as Pharaoh wants to see you immediately! Don't delay!"

What a shock, I quickly shaved myself, put on some fresh clothes because after all I was going before Pharaoh.

Trembling a bit, I was ushered in before Pharaoh, who was very agitated! The night before Pharaoh had two dreams which had greatly disturbed him.

It turned out, that he had sent for all the magicians and wise men of Egypt, but no one could interpret his dreams. He had told his cupbearer about his dreams.

Suddenly the cupbearer remembered me in prison, and how I had interpreted his dream! The cupbearer told Pharaoh, that he knew someone who could interpret his dreams. That person was Joseph, whom he had been in prison with! The cupbearer felt very bad that he had forgotten about me! And so he should have!

Pharaoh went on to explain his dreams to me and I told him that it was only God who can interpret dreams.

His dream was …

"He stood by the river. Suddenly out of the river came seven cows, fine looking and fat; and they were grazing in a meadow. Then, seven other cows came up after them out of the river, ugly and thin, and stood by the other cows on the bank of the river. The ugly and thin cows ate up the seven fine looking fat cows.

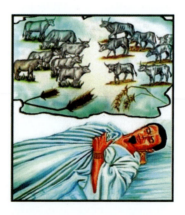

Pharaoh fell asleep again, and had a second dream. Suddenly seven heads of grain came up on one stalk, plump and good. Then, seven thin heads, scorched by the wind, sprang up after them. The seven thin heads devoured the seven plump and full heads."

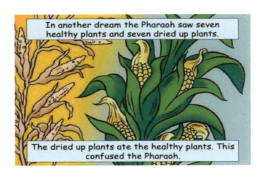

I began to tell Pharaoh, that the dreams he had been given were one and the same. God has shown Pharaoh what He was about to do. The seven good cows are seven years, and the seven good heads of corn are seven years. The seven thin and ugly cows which came up after them are seven years, and the seven empty heads destroyed by the scorching wind are seven years of famine.

God had spoken and shown Pharaoh what He was about to do. Seven years of great plenty will happen throughout Egypt, and then seven years of famine will follow. The famine will be very severe in Egypt, and the good years will be forgotten about.

The dream was repeated to Pharaoh twice because what God said would happen!

Pharaoh then asked me what he should do!

God showed me, and gave me specific instructions to tell Pharaoh. He was to choose a wise man, one who had the Spirit of God on him.

Pharaoh was to put the person in charge of Egypt with some assistants, to help him administer this very big project. They would need to gather enough grain during the seven years of abundance, in order to feed the nation of Egypt and surrounding countries during the seven years of famine! A job not for the faint hearted!

God gave me a specific strategy, as to how the seven years of abundance should be carried out.

One-fifth of the grain should be collected each year, during the seven plentiful years. The food must be gathered and stored up in huge grain storehouses. The food should be kept in the cities, until it was needed to be used to feed the people during the seven years of famine.

Prison To Prime Minister

Pharaoh was very quiet as he pondered this. After some time, I was summonsed again before Pharaoh and he told me I was the man for the job!

I was given the most senior job in Egypt and became the Prime Minister, because Pharaoh saw that God was with me and he could trust me.

Pharaoh gave me a lot of power and authority. He put a signet ring on my finger, gave me a robe and put a gold chain around my neck which was a sign of royalty. I rode all over Egypt in one of Pharaoh's chariots.

I was overwhelmed at the responsibility and challenge that lay ahead of me. I realised that all I had been through in my life was preparation for this moment. I gave my God, the God of Abraham and Isaac all the praise and thanks for raising me up for such a time as this.

I realised that I would need a lot of wisdom from God, and special leadership and administrative skills in order to carry out this task.

I was thirty years old when I became Prime Minister of Egypt. I was now beginning to fulfil my destiny, and the plans and purposes for which I had been created.

Dreams were beginning to be fulfilled. As time went by I married and had two sons called Manasseh and Ephraim.

I went out from the presence of Pharaoh, and went throughout Egypt to begin to fulfil my assignment.

In the seven plentiful years the ground was abundant. I gathered up all the food during the seven years which was in the land of Egypt, and stored the food in huge containers in the cities across the country. I gathered up as much grain, as I could, until we had to stop counting, because it was now immeasurable.

As God said would happen, the seven years of plenty which were in the land of Egypt ended, and then seven years of famine began.

The famine was very bad everywhere, and there was no food, but in Egypt there was plenty of food. When the famine began to take a grip in the country, and there was no food, all the people began to come to me begging for food.

I ordered that all the storehouses should be opened up and the grain sold to the Egyptians. The famine became very severe in the land of Egypt and all the surrounding areas. All the other countries started coming to Egypt to buy grain, because there was no food anywhere.

One day, I was standing outside the storehouse distributing the food, when suddenly I noticed a group of men coming towards me.

I instantly recognised them, but they didn't recognise me! I couldn't believe my eyes, but I never let on that I knew them! There were my brothers however, I noticed very quickly that Benjamin wasn't with them. They came towards me and bowed down to the ground, and asked me if they could buy sacks of food which they could take back to Canaan.

Suddenly, the dreams I had as a young man come flooding back, when I remembered the sheaths of corn that would bow down to me. Each of my brothers in turn bowed down before me.

I spoke to them in a cross manner as I wanted to test them. I pressed them with many questions, about my father and Benjamin. They looked surprised I was asking them so many questions. They went on to tell me, my youngest brother was with my father. I desperately wanted to see him again!

I accused them of being spies and trying to cause trouble, they assured me that was not the case, all they wanted was to purchase food for their families and go back to Canaan as quickly as possible!

However, I didn't believe them, so I had Simeon put in prison and told them to go home and bring my youngest brother back with them. Once I see him I will release Simeon and believe that they are not spies and trying to cause trouble!

They started talking in their own language and of course I understood every word, but I never let on that I understood what they were saying. They were very worried about Simeon staying, as our father had never got over the fact that I was probably dead! And now the possibility of losing another son!

It took them a long time to come back again, to buy more food, as my father knew that the next time they returned to Egypt they had to bring Benjamin with them, and he couldn't face letting Benjamin go.

However, the famine forced them to return and they brought my brother Benjamin with them, against my father's wishes. Apparently, my father was very distressed as he couldn't bear the thought of losing Benjamin as well as me!

Early one morning, I was standing distributing the food as usual. As I turned around I saw my brothers coming towards me, and there amongst them was Benjamin my favourite brother!

It had been so many years, since I had seen him. He was a young boy when I was sold by my brothers and now he was a young man. There had always been a special relationship between the two of us. I was longing to give him a hug!

I decided that I would take them back to the palace where I laid on a special meal for them. I arranged for their places at the table to be laid out in the order of their ages!

My brothers were staggered and looked at each other and still they didn't recognise me! They kept bowing down to the ground in front of me, and were wondering what was going to happen next!

Finally, I sent them on their way home back to Canaan to our father. I had arranged for extra food to be put in their sacks of grain.

However, I decided to test them again. I asked my steward to put my silver cup in the sack of food belonging to my youngest brother Benjamin. The next morning I asked the steward to chase after them and ask why they had stolen my silver cup!

My steward caught up with them and challenged them about stealing the cup. The steward made each of them, take their sacks off their donkeys and open them up. He checked them all starting with the eldest down to the youngest. He told them whoever's sack had the cup in it, would become a slave in the Palace and everyone else would be let off to go back home.

The cup was found in Benjamin's sack! Of course I knew that, as that was where I told the steward to put the cup. Apparently, they were all in shock and very afraid. They reloaded up their donkeys and returned to the city.

I was still in the Palace when they returned, and they begged me not to take Benjamin as a slave in the Palace. Their father had only allowed them to take Benjamin down to Egypt because I had insisted.

Benjamin was the only son my father had now from our mother Rachel. He thought that I had been killed and now to take Benjamin away would cause him to die of a broken heart. His heart was already broken but this would be too much to bear.

My brother Judah said that he would stay, but pleaded again and again with me not to keep Benjamin but let him go back to their father.

When I heard news of my father, how he was getting much older and he still missed me and thought of me every day! I could not control myself before them any longer.

I demanded that all my servants left me alone with my brothers, and I told them who I was! It is Joseph! All I wanted to know was that my father was still alive and in good health. My brothers could not answer me, for they were stunned into silence and became very afraid. I explained to them that it was me Joseph, whom they sold to the men from Midian and they had brought me to Egypt.

I explained to them that although they sold me and meant for evil things to happen to me, God has turned it around and was now using me to save their lives from starvation. He has made me Prime Minister of Egypt. I told them there was still another 5 years of famine but all would be well.

We all hugged each other and cried, and it was as though all the years of hurt from my brothers dropped away. I told them that they could all come and live in the land of Goshen with their families and livestock.

My brothers told me that they had to hurry back to my father as quickly as possible, and tell him the wonderful news that I was alive and God had prospered me and given me great favour in the land of Egypt.

Soon afterwards, Pharaoh got to hear that my brothers had arrived in Egypt, it caused quite a stir and everyone in the Palace got to hear about it.

I had gained great favour with Pharaoh. Pharaoh gave me wagons so that my brothers could go back to Canaan and collect my father and their families plus all their livestock.

Pharaoh promised to give my family the best land in Egypt where they could live, and that they weren't to worry about a thing as he would provide everything they needed.

I gave my brothers provisions for the journey, fresh clothes, extra money, but I gave Benjamin 5 times as much as the others because he was my very special brother!

When my brothers got back to Canaan they told my father all that they had seen and heard! He couldn't believe his ears. He couldn't believe that anything so wonderful could happen! However, when he saw all the wagons and the provisions he said, "I believe Joseph my son is still alive. I will go and see him before I die."

I was very busy as Prime Minister of Egypt, but I couldn't wait to see my father again. I longed for the time when I would see him and I knew it wouldn't be much longer.

Finally, I heard that they had left Canaan and were nearing Goshen where they would be living.

I climbed into my chariot and went out to meet my father. When we saw each other we hugged and hugged, and cried for joy, and relief to see each other again. It had been thirteen long years since I last saw him!

In time, Pharaoh requested to meet my father, so I arranged a meeting at the Palace with Pharaoh. Pharaoh promised to give my family, the very best place in Egypt to live and everything they needed would be provided.

The famine continued and got worse and worse but during this time everyone in Egypt had food. Because of the way I had been faithful and gathered the grain in the good years, there was always enough for everyone in Egypt, and the surrounding countries throughout the years of famine.

My father and all my brothers lived in Egypt for 17 years, before my father died. When I realised that my father was very old and his health was failing, I asked him to bless my two sons Manasseh and Ephraim.

Jacob laid his right hand on Ephraim's head, he was the younger, and his left hand on Manasseh's head (Manasseh was the eldest). In my eyes it was the wrong way round!

As my father was losing his sight I said to my father, "Not this way father, Manasseh is the firstborn, put your right hand on his head." My father refused and was insistent and said, "I know, my son, he shall become great. However, his younger brother shall be greater than the older brother, and his offspring shall become a multitude of nations." So he blessed them that day.

A father's blessing is very important in my culture it means more than anything in the world. My father was very old and drawing to the end of his life, and he blessed me and each of my brothers.

I will never forget the blessing he said over me.

My father told me that:

"I was a fruitful bough by a spring; my branches run over the wall. The archers bitterly attacked me, shot at me, and harassed me severely, yet my bow remained unmoved; my arms were made agile by the hands of the Mighty One of Jacob, by the God of your father who will help you, by the Almighty who will bless you with blessings of heaven above. May they be on your head and on your brow as you were set apart from your brothers...."

Soon after this time my father Jacob died, and was buried with his father Isaac and my grandfather Abraham. When he died, I missed him very much. He was truly the Patriarch in our family, as he held it together in many ways and he had walked in the ways of His God for many years.

Life continued for me in Egypt as did the famine for several more years.

I was so grateful that I was able to be reunited with my father again after all those years, and to spend time with him and talk about things that we hadn't been able to talk about for many years. He was able to see his grandchildren growing up, and he blessed me and my sons.

I was also able to spend time with my brothers again, and get to know them and make up for all the years when we were apart.

As I look back over my life, I can truly say that, through all the experiences, trials and tribulations of life, everything has worked together for good as I've trusted God to fulfil His plan and destiny for my life.

This can be your story too!

The End

2

MOSES

The Relucant Leader

The Israelites had been living in Egypt, since the time when Joseph was Prime Minister as there had been a very bad famine. They had prospered during this time and were getting very powerful.

The Pharaoh King of Egypt was a hard cruel man, and he was getting worried about how prosperous the Jewish people had become and the population was growing rapidly. He decided to send out an order that all Jewish baby boys, as soon as they were born, were to be thrown into the River Nile, because he was afraid that they might become too powerful. Only the baby girls would be allowed to live.

One day, a Jewish couple who were living in Egypt, at the time, had a little baby boy called Moses he was very special to them. They were afraid that someone would hear him crying and report on them, and the baby would be taken away and thrown into the River Nile.

His parents decided to hide him. Moses's mother made a little basket out of reeds which she wove together, and then lined the basket with a blanket. She painted the outside of the basket with tar and pitch. The reason she did this, was because when the basket was put in the river, it would float like a little boat, and wouldn't leak or sink!

She put her little baby boy inside the basket, then she and her husband went down to the River Nile. When no one was looking, she placed the basket with her precious baby amongst the reeds where he would be well hidden, but she could keep an eye on him!

Moses had a sister called Miriam, who was asked to keep a careful watch over her baby brother as well.

One day, Miriam was hiding by the river, watching her little brother, when all of a sudden one of Pharaoh's daughters came down to the River Nile to bathe. As she and one of her maids were walking along the riverbank, they noticed the basket among the reeds, so she sent her maid to go and fetch it out of the water. As she looked into the basket she saw it was a baby! He was crying and they wondered what he was doing in the river! They looked at each other and suddenly realised that this was one of the Hebrew babies!

Miriam gasped as she was peeping through the reeds, watching all that was going on. She quickly ran up to them and suggested that she went and found a nurse to look after the baby! Pharaoh's daughter thought this was a great idea, so Miriam rushed back home and found Moses's mother!

Baby Moses was brought back home safely to his family to be looked after. However, after a few years when Moses was a little older, his mother took him to Pharaoh's daughter who adopted him.

Moses grew up in the palace of Pharaoh and learnt all the ways of the Egyptians even though he was Jewish. He had many privileges growing up in a palace as well as the best education, clothes, food and everything he needed or wanted!

Despite growing up in a palace, and living amongst the Egyptians, Moses never forgot that he was Jewish a Hebrew. As time went by he saw the way the Egyptians treated the Hebrews, making them work long hours and very hard. One day, he came across an Egyptian beating a Hebrew and it made him so angry that he killed the Egyptian and then hid him in the sand trying to cover up what he had done!

Later on he saw two of his own people fighting and asked them what was wrong. Moses tried to stop them fighting but they had seen what he did to the Egyptian and thought he might kill them too!

Moses became afraid as he was sure everyone knew that he had killed one of the Egyptians! In fact Pharaoh got to hear that Moses had killed an Egyptian and wanted to kill him too. So Moses decided that it was best to run away into the desert for a while.

Moses was in the desert for a long time. After sometime he met and married his wife and had two sons. During this time he became a shepherd and looked after his father in law's sheep.

While Moses was in the desert, the king of Egypt died. The Israelites were slaves and being treated in a very cruel way and they were crying out to their God to be delivered. Had God forgotten them? Why hadn't God rescued his people?

It was just another day for Moses in the desert with his flock of sheep. He was wondering what he should be doing with his life, or if looking after sheep in the desert was all he had to look forward to?

It was a very hot dry day in the desert. Suddenly Moses looked up and noticed a bush was on fire but it wasn't getting burnt up!! He hurried over to the bush to investigate, as he had never seen anything like it before. Suddenly he heard a voice from inside the bush calling him, "Moses! Moses!" He was amazed because there was no other human being for miles!

Moses knew immediately it was God talking to him from the bush, but was amazed that God knew his name! He answered, "Here I am!"

God told him to take off his sandals, as he was standing on holy ground. God then said, "I am the God of your father, the God of Abraham, the God of Isaac and the God of Jacob." Moses was very afraid and covered his face with his cloak as he couldn't look at God.

God reassured him that he has seen the misery of His people in Egypt and heard their cry and was going to rescue them from the Egyptians. He was going to bring them up out of Egypt into a good and wonderful land, a land flowing with "milk and honey".

God told Moses that He was sending him to Pharaoh, in order that he could ask him to let His people go as it was time to bring them out of Egypt.

Moses was afraid about going to Pharaoh and started arguing with God and putting up obstacles.

God told Moses that He was going to be with him. Moses had a lot to say to God, and told Him that he couldn't speak very well and wasn't very good at expressing himself! Moses asked God to send someone else as he wasn't capable of standing before Pharaoh! Moses seemed to know what he couldn't do, but God knew what he could do!

The Lord wasn't very pleased with Moses, as he had specifically chosen Moses for the task of leading His people the Israelites out of their slavery in Egypt to the land of Canaan in Israel! However, the Lord told him he would allow his brother Aaron to go with him and speak to Pharaoh.

Moses was worried that Pharaoh wouldn't listen to him. God told him that if that was the case, He would give Moses the ability to perform signs in front of Pharaoh so that he would know that God has spoken.

One of the signs God gave Moses was that, as he threw his rod onto the ground it would become a snake in front of Pharaoh, and when he picked it up by the tail it would become a rod again.

So Moses went back home and said goodbye to his father in law and took his wife and children and went back to Egypt.

Although Moses was going back to face Pharaoh, he knew that God had spoken to him, and so with confidence he went back to Egypt knowing that God was going with him and would never leave him and give him the words to speak to Pharaoh.

When he got back to Egypt he met up with his brother Aaron and told him everything that had happened by the burning bush.

They also spoke to the Israelites and told them that God had seen their misery, and heard there cries and that he was going to bring them out of Egypt, and take them to the land of Canaan.

One day Moses and Aaron went to Pharaoh and told him, that the God of Israel says, "Let my people go to worship Me." Pharaoh was mocking and defiantly told Moses, that he would not let the Israelites go?

Pharaoh's heart became very hard towards the Israelites. He didn't want them to go because they were his labour force.

The Israelites were told to go and gather their own straw to make the bricks, as the straw would no longer be provided for them, but they must make the same number of bricks!

Ever since Moses and Aaron went to see Pharaoh the situation had become worse and worse. The Israelites were desperate and crying out to God to hear their cry and deliver them from this cruel man.

Moses and Aaron went back to Pharaoh again and again to ask him to let the Israelites go and worship their God.

God began to harden Pharaoh's heart, and He sent all sorts of horrible plagues on the Egyptians, but he protected the Israelites from every one of them.

The first plague God sent was to turn the River Nile into blood. Pharaoh still didn't believe it was from God.

So God sent the second plague of thousands of frogs! They were jumping everywhere, even in the Egyptians' houses and beds!

After the frogs, God sent a plague of gnats. They buzzed all around the people and animals driving them mad!

The fourth plague was a plague of flies. After the flies, God sent a horrible plague on all the Egyptians' horses, camels, and other animals, but God protected the Israelites' animals.

The sixth plague was a plague of boils. The Egyptians got big, painful sores on their skin. But Pharaoh still wouldn't free God's people! So God sent another plague of hail all over the land. The hail flattened and destroyed all their crops. Pharaoh said he would let the people go, but as soon as God stopped the hail, Pharaoh changed his mind and didn't let them leave!

God sent three more plagues, a plague of locusts (which are like grasshoppers), a plague of darkness (where the land was dark for 3 days).

Then the worst plague of all was that the firstborn in every household including the animals would die. Moses warned Pharaoh that the firstborn child of every family in Egypt would die if the Israelites were not freed! It was only when the final plague happened

Pharaoh finally let them go.

If Pharaoh had listened to Moses and obeyed God, none of these plagues would have happened to them.

It was a terrible night for the Egyptians when at midnight, an Angel sent by God passed through Egypt and killed every firstborn in every family as well as their animals. It happened as God said it would!

God promised the Israelites that no destructive plague would touch them. The Israelites were given very specific instructions. They were told to kill a lamb, and paint the blood of the lamb on the top and both sides of the doorframe, and to stay in their homes all night.

God promised that when He sees the blood on the door posts, He will pass over their homes and no disaster will come near them.

To this day the Jews celebrate the "Passover" when God passed by their homes but killed all the firstborn of the Egyptians. For seven days they eat bread made without yeast. On the first day they remove from their house all the bread and cakes that has been made with yeast. They don't go to school or work on these days. They prepare lots of different foods to eat as it is a time of celebration.

During the night Pharaoh summoned Moses and Aaron to the Palace and he told them to get out of Egypt immediately! Go Now! The Israelites had lived in Egypt for a very long time. About six hundred thousand men plus their wives and children, possibly about a million people and all their livestock left Egypt that day.

The Egyptians couldn't wait to get rid of the Israelites! They were nothing but trouble! The Egyptians had nothing left, their country, livestock and families had been completely destroyed!

Crossing the Sea

After the Israelites had fled, Pharaoh suddenly realised what he had done as all his labour force had gone! He decided to chase after them and bring them back! Pharaoh got six hundred of the best chariots to chase them! They chased them all day and night.

By this time, the Israelites had been walking for several days towards the Red Sea. Just when they thought they were safe, suddenly, they heard that the Egyptians were chasing after them and they had lots of chariots and horsemen! They were terrified but Moses told them not to be afraid! God is with us!

By now, the Israelites had reached the edge of the Red Sea. There was a huge sea ahead of them, and behind them the Egyptians were chasing them as hard as they could go! The Israelites looked at the Red Sea and the impossible situation – there was no escape! Were they all going to drown?

However God had a plan! He told Moses to stretch out his shepherd's staff over the sea to divide the water, and make a path through so that the Israelites could walk through the sea on dry ground.

As Moses stretched out his hand over the sea, the LORD divided the sea back with a strong wind and made a path of dry land. The Israelites and all their livestock walked through the sea on dry ground, with a wall of water on their right and on their left. It took quite a while for a million people and all their animals to walk through. Can you imagine walking along with a wall of sea water as high as you can see either side of you?!

The Egyptians were still chasing them, and by now Pharaoh's horses, chariots and horsemen had caught up with the Israelites! They started following them into the sea! The LORD saw the

Egyptians and threw them into confusion! He jammed the wheels of their chariots so that they had difficulty driving. Eventually the Egyptians said, "Let's get away from the Israelites! The LORD is fighting for them against Egypt."

Once all the Israelites and their animals had walked through the Red Sea, the LORD told Moses to stretch out his hand again over the sea so that the waters flowed back. As Moses stretched out his hand the water flowed back and covered the chariots and horsemen—the entire army of Pharaoh that had followed the Israelites into the sea. Not one of them survived!

That day the LORD saved the Israelites from the hands of the Egyptians. This is the biggest miracle that God did for the Israelites protecting them from their enemies.

The Israelites were in the desert on their way to the Promised Land for forty years! It could have taken about 8 days, but because of their disobedience, grumbling and rebellion it took a long time!

However, during that time God provided them with everything they needed. He provided water out of a rock when they needed it; fresh food called "manna" for them every day. Their clothes and sandals didn't wear out! He also provided a pillar of fire at night and a cloud by day to guide and protect them.

However, they made God very cross because all they did was complain, grumble and moan all day long. They even thought it would be better to be back in Egypt under the cruel Pharaoh! God got very cross with them! He had promised them a good life in Canaan, but they didn't believe Him!

On one occasion, they were travelling through the desert and it was very hot, but there was a problem because they had no water.

A million people and all their animals needed water! They complained and moaned to Moses so much that he got very fed up with them.

Eventually they came to a rock and God told Moses to speak to the rock and water would come out, but instead because Moses was so cross he struck the rock with his staff. Water gushed out of it, but God was not pleased with Moses and because of his disobedience in not carrying out God's instructions, he never reached the Promised Land and died in the desert.

One day Moses went up onto a very high mountain called Mt Sinai as God wanted to talk to him. Moses was up on the mountain for a very long time, as God was giving him the Ten Commandments. They were written on large tablets of stone by God.

The Ten Commandments

1. You shall have no other gods before me.
2. You shall not make for yourself an image in the form of anything in heaven above or on the earth beneath or in the waters below. You shall not bow down to them or worship them
3. You shall not misuse the name of the LORD your God, for the LORD will not hold anyone guiltless who misuses His name.
4. Remember the Sabbath day by keeping it holy. Six days you shall labour and do all your work, but the seventh day is a Sabbath to the LORD your God.
5. Honour your father and your mother, so that you may live long in the land the LORD your God is giving you.
6. You shall not murder.
7. You shall not commit adultery.
8. You shall not steal.
9. You shall not give false testimony against your neighbour.

10. You shall not covet your neighbour's house. You shall not covet anything that belongs to your neighbour.

When the people saw that Moses was a long time in coming down from the mountain, they asked Aaron to make them gods in an image who would lead them. We don't know what has happened to Moses. We can't wait any longer!

Aaron told them to take off their gold earrings and the jewellery they were wearing. Aaron took all the jewellery melted it down, and made an idol cast in the shape of a calf out of all the gold. He built an altar in front of the calf and they had a big party! Everyone was eating, drinking and worshipping the golden calf!

They thought that God couldn't hear or see what they were up to! God was very upset when He saw them all dancing before the golden calf because they weren't willing to trust and believe Him.

When Moses eventually came down from the mountain, he heard a lot of noise of celebrating and dancing, and saw the Israelites worshipping the golden calf!

Moses became very angry! He was so frustrated and cross with the Israelites, that he threw the tablets of stone down, with the Ten Commandments written on them, smashing them into pieces!

He took the calf the people had made and burned it in the fire! Then he ground it into a powder and put it in the water and made the Israelites drink the water!

MOSES

Sometime later, Moses went back up on to Mt Sinai with two large tablets of stone for God to write the Ten Commandments on them for the second time.

These large stones would later be kept in a special box in laid with gold called the Ark of the Lord. The Ark would be carried by the Israelites all the time they travelled through the desert.

As Moses was talking to God on top of the mountain, he told Him what a difficult time he was having leading this mob of disobedient Israelites. Moses was very honest with God, and God likes it when we are honest as to how we are feeling.

Moses reminded the Lord that the Israelites were His people. Moses needed reassurance that God was with him. The LORD told Moses, that He would never leave him, and that He would be with him as he led this rebellious bunch of people into the land of Canaan.

When Moses came down from the mountain again, he gave the people the new tablets of stone with the Ten Commandments the LORD had given him on Mt Sinai.

The Lord loved Moses very much and said he was the most humble man on the earth. Moses was the only person in the whole world that God spoke face to face with.

God loved being with Moses and Moses loved spending time with God, because Moses knew that the only thing worth having in life was being in God's Presence.

The End

3

DAVID THE SHEPHERD KING

I was born and lived in Bethlehem in Judea, which means "House of Bread". Bethlehem was about five miles from Jerusalem. It was a small but bustling village. I am David the youngest of my seven brothers. As a shepherd boy I looked after my father Jesse's large flock of sheep.

I would be out in the mountains and fields all day and every day, and often I was away for weeks at a time taking the sheep to fresh grazing. I slept out in the mountains and fields at night, so that I was always around ready to protect the sheep from any dangers.

Being a shepherd was a dangerous and skilled occupation, as often bears, lions and wolves would come down from the mountains to try and steal the sheep, and my job as a shepherd was to protect them. There were a lot of responsibilities as a shepherd. Every day the flock had to be checked, sometimes they injured themselves if they fell into a stream or went over a cliff edge. There were always new lambs being born and needing to be looked after.

I got very attached to the sheep and had my favourites! Of course there were always the naughty ones who wandered off and got lost or went somewhere they shouldn't have and had to be rescued!

I was a young man but very strong and had to learn how to kill wild animals if necessary. The only weapon I had was a spear and a sling. I would practise using my sling, and I played games to see how far I could aim and of course hit the targets.

There were several occasions when I had to kill a lion and a bear and even on one occasion a wolf with my bare hands. I had to kill them before they killed me and the flock of sheep I was protecting.

I loved being out in the countryside with the sheep, sleeping under the stars and enjoying the wonderful creation all around me. One of my favourite times was to lie on my back, in the pitch dark and gaze up at the masses of twinkling stars. It made me feel very close to the God of Israel.

In the winter it got very cold at night. I would light a small fire, to keep warm and also to keep the wild animals away. The only pillow and bedding I had was a rock and a blanket made from sheep's wool.

When I was quite young I developed a love for music. I remember my father asked the carpenter in our village to make me a harp. I taught myself and I would spend hours playing and strumming on my harp and composing songs.

My harp went with me wherever I went. As the sheep grazed, I would sit on a rock by a stream and play and sing. I would spend hours playing and reflecting on the beauty around me, and thanking the God of Israel, who I was brought up to love and respect. Thanking Him for his goodness and love to me.

One day, as I was sitting on my favourite rock, by a stream I started playing and singing songs, which I had composed. I would make up lots of songs and melodies singing them in the fields where no one heard me except the sheep! One of my favourites was:

The **Lord** is my Shepherd [to feed, to guide and to shield me] I shall not want.

He lets me lie down in green pastures,

He leads me beside the still *and* quiet waters.

He refreshes *and* restores my soul (life),

He leads me in the paths of righteousness for His name's sake.

Even though I walk through the [sunless] valley of the shadow of death, I fear no evil, for You are with me;

Your rod [to protect] and Your staff [to guide], they comfort *and* console me.

You prepare a table before me in the presence of my enemies. You have anointed *and* refreshed my head with oil;

My cup overflows.

Surely goodness and mercy *and* unfailing love shall follow me all the days of my life,

And I shall dwell forever [throughout all my days] in the house *and* in the presence of the **Lord**.

Often, I had to move the sheep down very difficult ravines at times passing through desert areas, negotiating tough terrain to get to the higher places where the good pasture land was.

It was a lonely and sometimes tough life, as my only companions for weeks on end were the sheep. All my friends and family were back in Bethlehem and I had no one else to talk to. Playing my harp and singing about God's goodness was a great comfort to me. I learned to talk to God, and experience His love in a way I would never have learnt to, if I had been in Bethlehem with all my friends and family.

The best part was that I was able to think about God, and talk with Him all day long, and he would talk to me and show me what to do.

I would often times, feel I had been forgotten by everyone. My father and brothers were busy with their lives in Bethlehem. Would I be a shepherd on my own in the mountains forever? I had plenty of time to think about my future and dream of what I would like to do when I was older?

If I had been away for a few weeks, and then came back home, I never felt very welcome. My brothers particularly, would prefer it if I was out of the way all the time!

One particular night, I had spent the night out in the mountains with the sheep. They were very restless that night, and as I walked around, I discovered a large bear trying to get in amongst the sheep. I threw my spear at him, and in spite of the dark and with fairly good accuracy, I caught him on his rump, which sent him growling and running as fast as he could go.

As I woke up early one morning, and watched the beautiful sunrise peeping up over the mountains, I had a song of joy in my heart and a sense of tremendous excitement.

I wondered what lay ahead of me this particular day, as it appeared to be like any other day. I was in the mountains on my own with the sheep all day? I got up and went down to the nearby stream to wash.

I had just started my routine of checking the sheep, when I looked up, and in the distance I saw one of my brothers coming towards me on his donkey. I wondered if something had happened to my father!

When he eventually arrived, he told me to come home immediately, as the Prophet Samuel had arrived in Bethlehem, to hold a special service, and had come to our house and was asking to see Jesse's youngest son!

I couldn't imagine why the Prophet Samuel would want to see me! I wasn't important, and after all I was only a shepherd boy!

Apparently, my father had laid on a special meal for the Prophet Samuel and my brothers, and they were waiting for me to arrive!

I whistled for the sheep, and we all hurried back to Bethlehem which fortunately wasn't too far away.

As I walked into the house, everyone was already seated at the table! As soon as I walked into the room Samuel stood up. The Lord had just spoken to him and told him, "Rise and anoint him, this is the one."

I knew from a young age that there was a big calling on my life, but I was shocked and not quite sure if what was happening to me was a dream! Samuel came over to me and took a horn of oil, poured it over my head, and anointed me to be King! This was done in the presence of my father and brothers! From that day on the Spirit of the LORD came upon me powerfully.

I knew that there was already a King over Israel called Saul, but I heard that he was very disobedient and God was displeased with him. He was no longer going to allow him to be King and I was going to be the King of Israel in his place!

Although I had been anointed to be King, it would be a long time before I actually became King of Israel. The people of Israel still recognised Saul as their King. Saul didn't know for a very long time, that I was the one who had been anointed King in place of him!

King Saul heard that I played the harp and sang, so one day he approached my father, and asked him if I would come and play my harp over him. Because the Spirit of the Lord had left King Saul, he was being troubled by all sorts of horrible things. My playing and singing helped Saul to become more calm and peaceful.

Saul liked me and asked me to become his armour bearer. I would carry his shield, spear and sword, from time to time when the king went before his army.

For a time, I went back to looking after my sheep where I was the happiest. Whilst I was still looking after my father's sheep war broke out between the Philistines and Israelites.

Three of my brothers went to join the army as the Israelites fought against the Philistines. The war went on for a long time.

Eventually, my father asked me to take some food and provisions to my brothers and make sure they were alright. I loaded up my donkey, and set off to where they were living. I arrived and eventually found my brothers but they didn't seem at all pleased to see me but enjoyed receiving the food I had brought with me!

While, I was talking to them a giant came out from the camp of the Philistines and shouted across the valley. He was daring someone to come from the Israelites' camp and fight with him.

The giant's name was Goliath. He was nine feet tall. His armour covered him from head to foot, and he carried a spear twice as long and as heavy as anyone could hold. His shield bearer walked before him, carrying his very heavy shield which must have weighed a tonne!

I heard that he had come out day after day for weeks, and called out across the valley, trying to intimidate and terrify the Israelites. He shouted out across the valley, "I am a Philistine, and you are servants of Saul. Now choose one of your men, and let him come out and fight with me. If I kill him then you shall submit to us, and if he kills me, then we will give up to you. Come, now, send out your man!"

The Israelites were terrified of this giant, and every time he came out they would be trembling with fear and back away and run back into their tents. Goliath was a big bully and made everybody afraid of him.

I asked my brothers why nobody had killed Goliath! They were rude to me and told me to go back and look after the sheep as I wasn't any use there, and what did it have to do with me!

One day, I decided that if no one else will go, I will go out and fight with this enemy of my people.

I was overheard saying this, and one of the men brought me before King Saul. King Saul hadn't seen me since I played my harp before him but he didn't recognise me which was surprising, as I hadn't changed that much!

Saul told me, that I couldn't fight with this great giant, because I am young and inexperienced, and he has been a man of war for many years.

I told King Saul that I may only be a shepherd, but I have fought with lions and bears, when they have tried to steal my sheep. And I am not afraid to fight with this Philistine.

Eventually King Saul agreed, I put on his armour but it was far too big for me and I could hardly move around in the heavy armour. So I decided to take it off.

I went away from all the noise and the crowds and asked the God of Israel what I should do? There was a little stream nearby, so I ran down and picked up five smooth stones and put them in the little pouch where I kept my sling, and also picked up my shepherd's staff.

The next day when Goliath came out with his taunting, I ran out to go towards him.

I thought may be the best way of fighting him, was to throw the giant off his guard, by appearing weak and helpless, and being further away from the giant he could not reach me first with his sword or spear. I decided to strike him down with a weapon which he would not be expecting or would not be prepared for!

I took my shepherd's staff in my hand, as though that was all I had. Out of sight, in a bag under my cloak, I had my five smooth stones carefully chosen, and a sling which I knew how to use very accurately.

The giant looked down on me in disgust and despised me. He laughed mockingly and said to me, "Am I a dog that this boy comes to me with a staff? I will give his body to the birds of the air, and the beasts of the field." The Philistine Goliath cursed me by his gods.

Trembling with excitement but with boldness and authority I shouted out to him, "You come against me with a sword, a spear, and a shield, but I come to you in the name of the Lord of hosts, the God of the armies of Israel. This day the Lord will give you into my hand. I will strike you down, and cut off your head."

I ran toward the Philistine, as if to fight him with my shepherd's staff! When he was just near enough for a good aim, I took out my sling, and hurled a stone aimed at the giant's forehead. My aim was perfect and the stone struck the Philistine in his forehead. It stunned him, and he fell to the ground stone dead!

While the two armies stood wondering, and scarcely knowing what had caused the giant to fall so suddenly, I ran forward, drew out the giant's own sword and cut off his head!

When the Philistines realised that their great warrior in whom they trusted was dead. They turned to flee back to their homes, and the Israelites followed after them, killing thousands of Philistines that day.

I had won a great victory and stood before everyone as the one who had saved his people from their enemies.

After I had killed the Philistine Goliath, the women came out from all the towns of Israel to meet King Saul. They were singing and dancing, with joyful songs with their tambourines and flutes. As they danced, they sang:

"Saul has slain his thousands and David his tens of thousands."

I had become a hero overnight, but this made King Saul very angry and jealous. From that time on my relationship changed with King Saul, as I realised that he hated me and wanted to kill me. Over the years, Saul tried several times to kill me even trying to use my best friend Jonathan to come against me.

Jonathan was Saul's son, and he had become my best friend. He was much closer to me than my own brothers, but Saul tried his hardest to break up my friendship with Jonathan which made me very sad.

I spent many years running for my life out of fear of King Saul. One of the reasons Saul hated me so much was because he saw the Spirit and favour of God on my life. The Lord had taken his hand off Saul and he was being troubled by lots of bad things.

There was war between the house of Saul and the house of David for a long time. I grew stronger and stronger, while the house of Saul grew weaker and weaker.

I became a mighty warrior and fought many battles and wars. I protected Israel from all her enemies. Everything I did I tried to enquire of God first as to what to do. Whatever God told me to do I tried to obey Him.

However, I made some very big mistakes in my life which caused me many problems over the years. In time my own children turned against me, and I had to flee for my life as my son Absalom wanted to kill his own father! I asked God to forgive me of all the wrong things I had done in my life! He did because He is a loving and faithful God.

One day there was another terrible war, and during that time King Saul and my best friend Jonathan were killed. Soon after that time I was anointed as King over Judah. God blessed me in every way. I was married and had a large family.

I love the God of Israel with all my heart and wanted to worship him with everything in me.

One very exciting day which I had been longing for, I heard that the Ark of God which is the place where the presence of God lives was being brought back to Jerusalem.

I was so excited, as it was a dream I had had in my heart for many years and now it was happening. The Ark had been captured by the Philistines and it brought the enemies of Israel a lot of trouble, and they wanted to get rid of the Ark and return it to Jerusalem where it belonged.

The Ark of the LORD would be placed inside a tent that I had made for it, and where my people would be able to make offerings of worship and thanks to the LORD.

The Ark of the Lord had accompanied the Israelites throughout their time in the desert, when they left Egypt to come to the land of Canaan. God's presence and His Glory dwelt in the Ark. The Ark was very important to the Jewish people and it had come back to Jerusalem where it belonged after many years.

As the Ark was being transported back into Jerusalem, I danced in the streets with everything in me together with all the people of Israel. However, my wife and many others laughed and mocked me, saying how undignified it was for a King to be dancing in the streets, but I didn't care as I wanted to bring honour, praise and thanksgiving to the Lord.

I was thirty years old when I became king, and I reigned in Israel for forty years. In Hebron, Judah I reigned for seven years and in Jerusalem for thirty-three years.

I became the greatest King Israel has ever had because the God of Israel was with me, and in spite of my mistakes His hand of favour was on my life, and also on the people of Israel.

During my reign, I had many victories and defeated many of Israel's enemies which included the Philistines; the Moabites; Ammonites, Arameans and many more.

Many years before I became King, when I was still looking after my father's sheep, I wrote lots of songs and these words have been very special to me through all the experiences of my life.

"The Lord is my rock, my fortress and my deliverer;

My God is my rock, in whom I take refuge."

There are many more stories about my life but these are just some of the highlights that have made me the person I am. I was known as the man after God's own heart.

The End

4

RUTH

Ruth is a young Moabite girl, growing up in a small insignificant village in Moab. However, Moab was a prosperous country with numerous natural resources. It was located along an important trade route to Egypt and Israel. There were friendly relations between Moab and Israel. Moab is a land which lies alongside much of the eastern shore of the Dead Sea.

Ruth's father is a farmer, who works very hard trying to produce a meagre income to sustain his large growing family.

Ruth is a pretty, active little girl with an outgoing personality. She has lots of friends in the village. She is expected to help her mother with the household chores of which there are many. Her main jobs each morning are to sweep the house, and gather sticks of wood for the fire. All the cooking is done on a small fire which is always kept going. The fire also heats the house during the winter months.

Ruth also has to look after her father's small flock of sheep, and take them up to the grassy meadows each day, and then bring them down each evening. She has to draw water for them from the well which is hard work. She draws bucket after bucket of water, as they seem to drink a lot. Finally, she puts them into their pen for the night.

Everyone in the family have their jobs to do, from helping their father on the farm; milking the cows; shearing the sheep and bringing in the wheat and barley harvests.

During the sheep shearing season Ruth gathers up all the wool. This needs to be washed and laid out on the rocks in the sun to dry. Ruth will then combe all the wool, so that the nettles and briars caught in the wool can be removed. It is a long process and then the last stage, Ruth will spin the sheep's wool into thread. After all this is done, Ruth's mother uses the thread to make blankets or rugs. It is a long and arduous job but very important. Some of the wool will get sold and the rest made into rugs and blankets for the family. Nothing gets wasted!

Ruth is a Hebrew name which means - compassionate; friend; vision of beauty. As Ruth grows up, she wonders what will happen to her, and what the future will hold.

She will be expected to marry young, and will probably be married off to one of the local boys from the village. She pondered this, and her thoughts went to a boy in her class called Deshan. He is a nice boy but he is quite full of himself. Also there is Moshe, she rather likes him but he didn't seem too interested in her! She often sits and daydreams about her future.

Her parent's marriage was an arranged one, as is the custom of everyone in her village, so she knows hers will be arranged too before she is much older!

At the end of the day, it will depend on her father, who she marries, and it will probably be one of the local boys, or, maybe, it could be someone from another village.

She hopes that her parents will make a good choice and that it won't be just a financial arrangement! However, her parents are poor, so her chances will not be very good, and it is most unlikely that she will marry into a wealthy family!

Her prospects will be to marry young, raise a family and that will be as much as she can look forward to. She hopes she will have a happy marriage and comfortable way of life.

The deep longing and unspoken feeling is that she wants something more, but not quite sure what. She wants her life to count for something. Although, she loves her home and village, she is sure that there must be something beyond the country of Moab, but the chances of ever leaving are not even an option. She can but dream!

One day, she went down to the well as usual to draw water for her mother. Several of the women from the village were also there washing clothes and chatting. Ruth overheard them saying that a new family has just moved into their village. They have come from Bethlehem in Judah to Moab because of the famine which was very bad there. They want to make a new life for themselves in Moab.

It has been a long time since a family, moved into their village but never someone from outside Moab before.

The villagers weren't too sure of these foreigners and it took them quite a while to accept them. As time went by it was as if they had always been there.

The family were from Bethlehem. They are called Elimelek and Naomi and their two sons are Mahlon and Kilion. The family became very friendly with Ruth's family, and as time went by Mahlon started helping Ruth's father on the farm. Mahlon became a frequent visitor to Ruth's home.

As Ruth grew older she was becoming very beautiful. Mahlon started to notice this beautiful young girl and began to fall in love with her. He was quite a bit older than Ruth, but the more she saw and talked to him, the more she fell in love with him too! They would try and spend as much time together getting to know each other.

After a while the two fathers began to discuss their children's marriage plans. Very soon it was all decided and arranged! A good financial agreement was also drawn up!

Mahlon is Jewish, and his God is the God of Israel, and he is going to marry a Moabite who will be a worshipper of Baal (which is idolatry worship). However, when Ruth marries she will be required to become Jewish like her husband.

After some time Ruth and Mahlon married and they were very happy. Kilion, Mahlon's younger brother also married a Moabite woman called Orpah.

Ruth and Mahlon lived with Elimelek and Naomi and during that time Ruth developed a special relationship with her mother-in-law Naomi.

Mahlon started farming and was able to obtain his own small piece of farm land. He also had a large flock of sheep and goats. Life was beginning to become a bit more prosperous for the family.

Mahlon's father Elimelek grew vegetables, and every week Mahlon helped his father take the vegetables to market, this was an important source of income for the family. As Elimelek was getting older, Mahlon was hoping to take over his father's business.

However, after several years Naomi's husband Elimelek suddenly died! It was a very sad time and everything changed for Naomi!

Naomi was now a widow and life would become very hard for her. However, she still had her two sons and their wives which was a great comfort to her. Mahlon took over the running of the vegetable farm as well, which meant that there would still be a small income for Naomi.

About 10 years later, very sadly both Naomi's two sons Mahlon and Kilion also died! It was a very difficult time for the families.

Naomi, Ruth and Orpah were now widows, and neither Ruth nor Orpah had children, which would only mean a very hard life ahead for them.

Naomi had not only lost her husband but also her two sons!

Things were desperate for these three women! What now? What of the future?

After all this sadness, Naomi decided she was tired of living in a foreign country amongst foreign gods. It was time to go back to her homeland which was Bethlehem in Judah and to her God the God of Israel.

She discussed her decision with her daughters-in-law Ruth and Orpah. They both decided that they wanted to go with Naomi. However, Naomi encouraged her daughters in law to go back to their family homes. She wanted them to remarry and find happiness again. Orpah decided to listen to her mother-in-law and went back to her family and stayed in Moab.

Ruth couldn't bear to leave her mother-in-law, and said that, wherever she went Ruth would go with her. She wouldn't listen to Naomi and insisted on going with her to Bethlehem.

Ruth also wanted to leave Moab as there has been so much sadness and she wanted to start a new life in Bethlehem. Although for her everything would be new, she was young enough to adjust to a new country, a new way of life and make new friends.

Naomi and Ruth packed up their belongings and started on the long journey back to Bethlehem. She and Naomi waved good bye to their family and friends. Ruth's family tried so hard to persuade her to come back and live with them but she had made up her mind. There was nothing for her in Moab anymore.

The two women set off on their long journey to Bethlehem. Naomi's life had turned out very differently, from how it had started out, when she set out for Moab from Bethlehem several years before with her husband and two sons.

Ruth's love, friendship and kindness brought much joy to Naomi and in time, Naomi began to forget about all her sadness and started to move on in her life.

In spite of Ruth's heathen background and the idol worship of Moab, Ruth became a follower of the true God of Israel, and she realised that bowing down to idols made of stone and wood, was so empty and worthless.

When Naomi and Ruth arrived in Bethlehem, many of Naomi's friends and relatives were still there and they gave her a loving and warm welcome.

Although, Ruth was also a widow she was happy and full of her new love in Jehovah. She was full of expectation and hope of her new life in Bethlehem.

Life was difficult when they first arrived, however, Ruth knew that she was going to have to go out to work as Naomi and Ruth must live. Ruth was a loving and thoughtful person, and knew that her mother-in-law was not able to work.

Fortunately, when they arrived it was the wheat and barley harvests, and the sheaves of corn were being gathered in, which meant that the farmers would be looking for people to work in their fields to help bring in the harvests.

One day soon after they arrived in Bethlehem, Ruth and Naomi were discussing where Ruth could work. Naomi suddenly remembered that one of her husband's relatives, was a very wealthy landowner, and he would also be reaping his fields at this time of the year. His name was Boaz.

Naomi told Ruth, which fields belonged to Boaz. Early one morning, Ruth went down and started picking up the corn in the field that the reapers had left behind them.

Boaz arrived back soon after Ruth had started working in his field. He immediately noticed her and wanted to know who she was. Boaz was told that Ruth had come to Bethlehem from Moab, with her mother in law, Naomi, so that she could look after her. He was very impressed with her love and kindness to Naomi, and was determined to make sure that she was well looked after as long as she worked in his fields.

Ruth worked hard all morning in the hot sun, and managed to gather a large armful of corn. She was hoping to gather as much as possible to take back to her mother in law.

Ruth had just sat down under a tree by herself when Boaz walked over to her! She was very concerned that he would be cross with her, because she was working in his field without permission. As he spoke to her, he was very kind and gentle and invited her to come and join them for lunch! Ruth was amazed at the favour she was receiving as a foreigner in a foreign country.

Ruth felt drawn to this man, after all he was a distant relative by marriage, and she wanted to get to know him! Ruth watched how kindly Boaz spoke to his workers. Boaz was very well respected in the town and he was also very wealthy landowner!

At the end of the day, when she had finished gathering her corn, she went to the threshing floor with all the other workers to thresh the corn she had gathered.

She was very happy when Boaz invited her to keep coming back each day, until the end of the harvests, which would last for about 3 months. She was grateful as this would provide food for herself and her mother in law.

As time went by, Ruth realised that this was the favour of the God of Israel whom she had recently come to know. Little did Ruth realise that God had directed her steps to the very field which in time would cause her to move into her destiny.

It was coming towards the end of the harvest season, and the workers were beginning to winnow the grain they had collected. This process needed to be done at night in the cool, and not during the heat of the day. The grain is thrown up into the air and caught in a big sieve. As it is thrown up into the air the wind catches it and all the bits that aren't any good are blown away, and only the best kernels are kept.

This is an important task as all the weeks of reaping the harvest are now being winnowed. The owner of the field normally spends the nights on the threshing floor to supervise things, as this is his profit for the year and wants to ensure that a good job is done.

One night Boaz had been working hard, he was tired and decided to lie down on his mat on the floor for a little sleep.

That particular evening Ruth, decided to go down to the threshing floor, she saw Boaz asleep in the corner and went and lay across his feet.

This was a position how Eastern servants frequently slept, if they were in the same tent with their master. If they needed a covering, custom allows them to share part of the covering of their master's bed.

Suddenly, during the night Boaz woke up and found Ruth at his feet, as it was dark he wasn't quite sure who it was! She told him, "I am Ruth your handmaid spread your robe over me, for you are my redeemer relative!" This act showed a real sign of humility on the part of Ruth before Boaz.

Boaz was Ruth's almost nearest relative and as was the custom in those days, he would be obliged to marry Ruth. Boaz was older than Ruth and he was impressed that she didn't want to marry a younger man.

However, there was a bit of a problem, as Ruth discovered that she had a relative, whom she had never met, who was an even closer relative than Boaz. As was the custom he would be next in line to marry Ruth.

Boaz was held in high regard by the men of the city, and so he decided to go up to the gate of the city, which consisted of a roofed building with no walls. It was the place where, in many Eastern towns all business transactions are made. Boaz took with him ten men who were elders of the city as witnesses.

Boaz wanted to marry Ruth as he really loved her. He needed to discuss this matter with the other relative. After discussions, with the other relative, and in front of the 10 elders who were witnesses, it was decided that it wouldn't be in his best interests financially to marry Ruth, as he would have too much to lose!

The deal was made in favour of Boaz much to his relief and delight! This now made it legal for Boaz to be able to marry Ruth!

In those days when a deal or transaction was made, one person took off his sandal and gave it to the other person which made the transaction legally binding.

Boaz married Ruth and they were very happy. After some time, Ruth had a baby boy whom they called Obed. Naomi her mother in law, was now very happy and fulfilled, as she had a little grandson whom she could love and spoil!

Ruth and Boaz fulfilled their destiny which they were created for, by obeying and waiting for God to work things out for them in His perfect way and timing.

Ruth and Boaz's son Obed would become the grandfather of the famous King David. Jesus many years later would be born into King David's family line.

Only God knew the role that Ruth and Boaz would play as they became part of Jesus family line.

The End

5

QUEEN ESTHER

I was living in Jerusalem in the land of Israel. My parents died when I was very young, and my cousin Mordecai who was like a father to me adopted me as one of his own. My Hebrew name is Hadassah which means Esther.

One day, I was snatched away from my homeland Jerusalem in Israel, and taken as a slave to Babylon by King Nebuchadnezzar who was the King of Babylon.

It was a frightening time as we didn't know what was going to happen to us. Fortunately, I was taken with my cousin Mordecai who tried to protect me and looked after me. My cousin Mordecai was also taken as a slave.

Babylon was situated on the Euphrates River, about 50 miles south of Baghdad which is now modern day Iraq.

Once we arrived in Babylon, I was taken into the King's Palace as part of his harem. I was young and growing into a very beautiful young lady so Mordecai kept telling me! Mordecai was given a job as a guard at the Palace.

Several months before I arrived, there had been a lot of trouble in the Palace. The Queen had made the King very angry and he had told her to leave the Palace and never return. The King was now looking for a new Queen!

As part of the King's harem before a young woman's turn came to be presented to King Xerxes, she had to complete twelve months of beauty treatments, six months with oil of myrrh and six with perfumes and cosmetics. It was a long but rather luxurious process!

The girls would be summoned to the Palace one at a time to be presented to the King and then return to the harem. She would not return to the king unless he was pleased with her and summoned her by name.

I had just completed my twelve months of beauty treatment, which made me feel wonderful! I had six months of treatment using the purest of oils one of which was Myrrh. This was followed by another six months of perfumes and cosmetics. I so enjoyed being pampered with different oils and perfumes. I should have looked good after all that treatment!

One morning, the attendant who was responsible for looking after the King's harem, told me that today it was my turn to go before the King. I felt very nervous and just wondered if he would approve of me! I had many thoughts and questions going through my mind. What would the future hold for me if he didn't approve? What would my future look like if he did approve?

I had never told anyone that I was Jewish because that would have gone against me. Babylon was a heathen country they believed in idol worship and I worshiped the God of Israel.

From the time I arrived in Babylon, I knew that the God of Israel was with me, I seemed to win the favour of everyone who saw me. My turn finally arrived to be taken before King Xerxes in his royal residence. I said goodbye to the other girls, whom I had become friends with, as I was taken off to the Palace.

On arriving at the Palace I was summoned in before the King. King Xerxes looked rather terrifying sitting on his throne, dressed up in all his robes with a crown on his head. He also held a long golden sceptre in his hand. I went forward trembling but with a tremendous sense of excitement.

After what seemed like ages, I left feeling a great sense of relief but also a sense of excitement of what lay ahead. I couldn't really imagine what the future held but knew that all would be well.

I heard later that the king was attracted to me more than any of the other girls, and I had won his favour and approval above everyone.

In time, King Xerxes told me that I was going to become the new Queen. I felt very humbled and was overwhelmed and honoured to be given such a role and responsibility. King Xerxes put a royal crown on my head and I became Queen. I was now the Queen of Persia.

A huge banquet was laid out in my honour with all his nobles and officials. He then proclaimed a holiday throughout the provinces and distributed gifts to everyone.

As soon as I could, I wanted to tell Mordecai myself about the honour that had been given to me. However, he already knew as the news had spread very fast round the Kingdom that I was the new Queen.

One day soon after I became Queen, Mordecai was sitting at the doorway to the Palace, and he overheard two of the King's security officials, who also guarded the palace discussing King Xerxes. They were very angry with him for some reason, and decided that they were going to assassinate him.

As soon as Mordecai found out he managed to get a message to me. I was shocked and immediately, went into the King to tell him of this news, and told him that Mordecai had informed me of this. The King sent for his private secretary, to investigate the story which proved to be true. The two officials were executed there and then. The King made a note in his journal that Mordecai had protected him and should be honoured in some way.

After sometime, King Xerxes decided to promote one of his staff called Haman to one of the most senior positions in the Palace.

Mordecai told me that Haman was a very arrogant man, and expected everyone to bow down to him when they were in his presence. Mordecai refused to do this which made Haman furious. Haman became so angry that he wanted to kill Mordecai.

Haman had discovered that Mordecai was Jewish, and decided that a much better plan would be to kill all the Jewish people who lived in Babylon. Haman hated the Jewish people and was a very wicked man.

One day, Haman asked for a meeting with the King and decided to spread horrible stories about the Jewish people. He told the King that they didn't obey his instructions and spread all sorts of lies. Everything he told the King about the Jewish people was untrue. Haman asked the King for his permission to destroy the Jewish people, as they weren't obeying the King's instructions.

So that day Haman, an enemy of the Jews, plotted against the Jews to destroy them. He cast the *"pur"*, which is similar to casting a dice for their ruin and destruction. The King agreed to this wicked plan without first checking to see if all the facts were true!

This wicked plan was put into place, and a letter was sent out, with the King's seal on it, and was distributed throughout all the provinces. The order was to destroy and wipe out all the Jews! Everyone would be killed young, old, men, women and children all on the same day. It was a very wicked plan. The day agreed was the thirteenth day of the month of Adar (which falls between February and March). Adar is one of the months in the Jewish calendar.

The letter was delivered by horseback across all the provinces. The Jewish people were very frightened and helpless, as they were being accused of all sorts of things they hadn't done.

Haman was delighted that his wicked plan was being carried out. He wanted to get revenge on the Jewish people because he hated them so much.

A few days had lapsed, before Mordecai discovered about this plan of Haman's. He was distraught and prayed to the God of Israel about what he should do to try and intervene with this plan. Many Jews had already received the letter and they were distressed and afraid.

Soon after this, it was brought to my attention that Mordecai was very upset, so I sent one of my officials to find out what the problem was. When the report came back to me, I was very disturbed, because after all, Mordecai and I were both Jewish. I was given a copy of the letter that had been sent out.

Unbeknown to me the King had agreed to this wicked plan, and of course the King didn't know that I Queen Esther was also Jewish.

I was very upset that the King had agreed to this plan, and had never mentioned it to me. I hadn't seen the King for a month now! Mordecai sent me a message, begging me to go before the King and ask for this plan to be stopped immediately.

I was very concerned about going before the King uninvited, but I was desperate for my people to be saved. I pondered this for several days, then I reminded Mordecai through my official, that anybody, who approaches the king without being summoned by him can be put to death, unless the king extends the golden sceptre to them and then their lives are spared.

My words were reported back to Mordecai. He sent a reply and told me very firmly, that I had a responsibility, to do something about the situation. Just because I am living in the king's palace didn't mean that I would escape! He went on to tell me that, if I remained silent at this time, relief and deliverance for the Jews will come from somewhere else, and I and my family will perish. He felt that I have come to my royal position for such a time as this!

I quickly sent back an instruction to Mordecai to gather together all the Jews who are in Susa, (which is the name of the province we live in) and to fast with me. No one is to eat or drink for three days, night or day. I and my attendants will fast too. When this is done, I will go to the king, even though it is against the law. And if I perish, I perish!

Mordecai went away and carried out all of my instructions. My attendants and I began a three day fast, and I prayed to the God of Israel to protect my people, and to give me favour as I went before the King.

I asked God to give me a strategy, as to the best way of approaching the King, as I hadn't seen him for a month and needed his favour.

On the third day of my fast, I had my plan and I knew what I was going to do! I decided that when I went before the King, I would invite Haman and the King to a banquet which I would hold in their honour.

I called my officials and asked them to prepare a lavish banquet today for the King and Haman.

I quickly, called my attendants to help me dress up in my royal robes. I put the King's favourite perfume on, and went and stood in the inner court of the palace, right in front of the king's hall.

I could see the king sitting on his royal throne in the hall, facing the entrance. As he looked up, he saw me standing there, my heart was beating very fast, but I could see he looked pleased to see me.

What a relief! He suddenly held out the golden sceptre towards me. Very relieved and trembling a little I approached the King and touched the tip of the sceptre, as one did when approaching the King. He asked me, "What is it, Queen Esther? What is your request? I will give you up to half of my kingdom." I asked the King, if he and Haman would like to come today to a banquet that I had prepared for them both in their honour.

The King appeared delighted and sent a message to Haman inviting him to come to the banquet. As we were all eating and drinking, the King turned to me and asked me what my request was? He was very intrigued and wondered what was on my mind.

To their surprise, I decided to invite them to another banquet the following day! I told him that I would answer his question then. The King was left in suspense for another day!

Haman was over the moon that he had been specially invited to the banquet I was giving. I heard that he boasted about this to anyone who would listen to him!

As Haman went home that day, he boasted to his wife about how wonderful he was! He was so prosperous, had a large family and everything was going very well for him or so he thought!

Mordecai continued to insist on not giving Haman any respect and this infuriated Haman even more. Everyone knew how much Haman hated Mordecai.

Haman was planning wicked things against Mordecai as well, and was becoming more and more filled with hatred against him.

Haman discussed the situation with his wife and his friends, who encouraged him to do away with Mordecai!

They suggested having a huge set of gallows built in their back garden, and ask the king if Mordecai could be executed on them the next morning.

As Haman was a senior official in the Palace, he felt that whatever he suggested to the king would be granted. Haman was delighted at this plan. Another plan was set in place which was about to work! Or so he thought!

That night back in the Palace the King was unable to sleep. He tossed and turned all night and was very disturbed. He got up the next morning and asked for his journals to be brought to him. These journals contain all the events that have happened during his reign so far. As he was looking through them he noticed an occasion, several years before, when Mordecai had reported two officials who wanted to kill him. He remembered that he had wanted to honour Mordecai for this, but it appeared that nothing had ever happened.

The King called in his attendants, and reminded them of the incident and checked with them if anything had been done to honour Mordecai. Apparently, nothing had been done. The King was determined that this should be rectified immediately.

Just at that moment Haman arrived at the Palace, as he was planning to discuss the execution of Mordecai with the King.

Haman was called in to see the King who asked him, "What should be done to the man the king delights to honour?"

Now Haman was a hard and arrogant man, and he thought to himself, who is there that the king would rather honour than me! He immediately answered the king, and said that a royal robe the king has worn should be put on him, and he should be given a horse that the king has ridden. He should also be paraded through the streets and honoured in this way.

The king was delighted at this suggestion and commanded Haman, to go at once and get the robe and the horse and do just as he had suggested for Mordecai the Jew!

Haman went pale with shock and anger. The king had spoken so there was nothing more to discuss!

Haman went out of the King's presence furious! He found Mordecai and brought him up to the Palace. In front of the King, he put the royal robe on Mordecai and led him on horseback parading him through the streets, and declaring that this is what is done for the man the king delights to honour!

Mordecai was a humble man. He was honoured and delighted that at last, he was being acknowledged for what he had done several years before.

Haman rushed home in fear and panic. He told his wife and all his friends what had happened. Haman's family realised that, coming against the Jewish people would be his downfall and things were going to go from bad to worse for him and the whole family.

Haman was discussing the terrible things that had happened that morning, when an official came to summon him to the banquet which had been laid on for him and the King by Queen Esther.

He had completely forgotten about the banquet, and it was the last thing in the world that he wanted to do! He quickly changed and rushed up to the Palace. He had to smile and pretend everything was just fine, as one couldn't be miserable in the King and Queen's presence.

The King and Haman came to my banquet, and as we were drinking and eating once again, the king again asked me what my request was? He assured me that it would be granted!

I boldly began to tell him my problem, as I had nothing to lose! If he refused it and it cost me my life so be it! I would have at least tried to save my nation.

I explained to him that my people, the Jewish people had been sold to be destroyed, killed and wiped out! I went on to say that, if we had just been sold as slaves, I would have kept quiet and not

QUEEN ESTHER

bothered the king, but an order has gone out to destroy and wipe out the Jewish people.

The King was outraged and demanded to know immediately who had given this order? Where is he! How dare anyone do such a thing? I pointed to Haman who sat there quivering, and looking as though he was about to faint! I told the king that it was the wicked man sitting in front of him called Haman!

The arrogant puffed up Haman, suddenly became a quivering wreck before the King and I. The King stormed out of the Palace very angry. I think Haman already knew what was going to happen to him! I was sitting on my couch and Haman came towards me on bended knee begging me to save his life! At that moment the King came back in and saw him pleading with me to save his life. King Xerxes immediately threw him out of the Palace and demanded that he was taken away.

Two of the King's officials came in and took Haman off. They roughly grabbed him and dragged him outside. As the officials were leaving with Haman, they informed the King that a very tall set of gallows had been erected in Haman's back garden and these had been intended for Mordecai!

King Xerxes issued an order that Haman would be executed on the very gallows, that he had intended for Mordecai!

As a result, Mordecai was promoted to a high position in the Palace. I then told the King that I was related to Mordecai.

After all the commotion with Haman had calmed down, I again pleaded with the king, and cried asking him to put an end to the evil plan of Haman's which he had organised against the Jews.

I requested that an order be written overruling the instructions that Haman had written to destroy the Jews in all the king's provinces. I cried saying that I couldn't bear to see disaster and destruction fall on my people the Jews.

King Xerxes extended the golden sceptre again to me. He instructed that another order was to be written out in the king's name on behalf of the Jews and seal it with the king's signet ring—for no document written in the king's name and sealed with his ring can be changed.

With a great flurry, as there was no time to lose, the royal secretaries were summoned. They wrote out Mordecai's orders to the Jews in all the King's provinces. These orders were written in the language of each province. Mordecai wrote in the name of King Xerxes, and sealed the letter with the king's signet ring.

The couriers, riding the royal horses, went out, hastened on by the king's command. As the letter arrived in people's homes in every province across the Kingdom, there was great happiness, joy, and gladness among the Jews! There was a lot of celebrating!

On the thirteenth day of the month of Adar, the instruction commanded by the king was to be carried out. The enemies of the Jews who had hoped to overpower them, now had the tables turned, and the Jews got the upper hand over those who hated them.

The Jews assembled in their cities, in all the provinces of King Xerxes, to attack those determined to destroy them. No one could stand against them, because the people of all the other nationalities were afraid of them. All Haman's sons were also killed that day.

Mordecai had become one of the most important people in the palace; his reputation spread throughout the provinces, and he became more and more powerful. In fact he became second in command to King Xerxes.

From this time on, until today, Jews have celebrated Purim, which is a time of celebration, joy, throwing parties and giving presents, to thank the God of Israel that the evil Haman was destroyed and that his wicked plan never happened.

Haman, the enemy of all the Jews, had plotted against the Jews to destroy them and had cast the *"pur"* which is similar to casting a dice for their ruin and destruction.

Through the help and wisdom of the God of Israel He enabled me to save an entire nation! This took a lot of courage and faith, but this only happened as I was willing to trust God and risk my own life for my people the Jews.

As I looked back over my life, I realised that everything that had happened to me, being taken as a slave from Jerusalem to Babylon; landing up in the King's harem; going before the King receiving his favour, and the timing of becoming Queen of Persia, were all the reasons that I was born for a time such as this.

The End

6

DANIEL

King Nebuchadnezzar, King of Babylon attacked Jerusalem and surrounded the city and captured many Israelites and brought them back to Babylon.

The young Daniel was among the Jews who were captured and brought to Babylon, (which today is in Iraq) from Jerusalem after Nebuchadnezzar conquered the city.

The chief official for King Nebuchadnezzar was instructed to look for handsome, intelligent, well-trained, educated young men who were quick to learn, to see if they would qualify to serve in the royal court. They needed to come from noble families.

Daniel was a handsome, intelligent young man who came from a noble family. He was one of those selected to go on a three year training programme to see if he would qualify for service in the royal court. He met all the requirements together with three other young men called Shadrach, Meshach, and Abednego.

Daniel, Shadrach, Meshach, and Abednego amongst other young men, had been enrolled on the three year training programme in order to be fit to serve in the royal court.

They would also be required to learn to read and write in the Babylonian language. The King's chief official was instructed that they must have the very best of everything including the foods and wines served from the royal table.

Daniel was a very brave young man who had strong convictions, and wasn't afraid to follow them through and speak out when necessary.

Daniel decided that he and his three friends weren't going to eat the food from the royal table. Daniel prayed and asked His God, for favour as he approached the chief official who was in charge of them. Daniel told him that they didn't want to eat the rich foods and wines, but asked if they could be given vegetables and water! The chief official was very worried, as he would be disobeying the King's instructions.

His concern was that Daniel and his three friends wouldn't look as fit and well as the other young men if they only ate vegetables and water. If the King found out he could lose his job and may be worse!

Daniel suggested that they try their diet of vegetables and water for 10 days, and then compare them with the other young men who were going to eat the food from the royal table.

After the ten days the Chief Official, looked at them, and agreed that they looked healthier and stronger than the others who had been eating the royal food! So they were allowed to continue eating vegetables and water instead of what the king provided.

God gave these four young men supernatural knowledge and skill in literature and philosophy. To Daniel he gave special skills in interpreting visions and dreams. He was quickly recognized by everyone in Babylon for his devotion to the one God.

After three long years, all the young men being trained up, including Daniel, Shadrach, Meshach, and Abednego were presented before King Nebuchadnezzar. Out of all the young men presented to the King, Daniel and his three friends impressed the King the most and they were offered positions in the King's court.

Daniel and his friend's hearts were following after their God and although they were living in a heathen country, they never allowed this to affect them, as they obeyed the God of Israel. Everybody could see that the favour of God was on their lives.

Daniel was held in high respect and he was considered one of the wisest men of the court of Babylon. Officials in the royal court knew that there was something different about Daniel, as he carried an authority and standard of excellence. Daniel knew it was because of his God. Daniel and his three friends were gaining in power and status in the King's court.

However, one day King Nebuchadnezzar decided to build a golden statue. It was huge ninety feet high and nine feet wide. Everyone was instructed to attend, a special service to unveil the statue where a large orchestra would be playing. The King also issued an order instructing, everyone, wherever they were, as soon as they heard the orchestra strike up to bow down and worship the golden statue. If they didn't they would be thrown into a blazing furnace!

Babylon was a heathen country and they followed heathen gods and customs. Daniel and his three friends were very distressed by this announcement. They knew they could never bow down to a golden statue, as they followed and believed in the God of Israel.

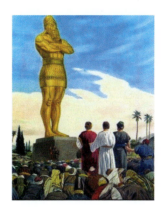

Everyone in the royal court knew that Daniel and his three friends were Jews. There were some officials who didn't like the Jews and wanted to cause trouble so they told the King that, Shadrach, Meshach, and Abednego hadn't bowed down to worship the golden statue when the orchestra started up.

When the king was told that three of his senior officials were being disobedient, and not bowing down to the statue, he was outraged and ordered the men to be brought to him. They were summoned before the king, as he wanted to make sure that it was true, that they had refused to worship his god and to bow down to the golden statue that he had set up?

These three were his most trusted and respected officials, so the King decided to give them another chance! The orchestra started up and all eyes were on Shadrach, Meshach, and Abednego he told them that if they didn't bow down they would immediately be thrown into a blazing furnace. The King mocked them, telling them that their God wouldn't be able to save them now.

I wonder what was going through the minds of Shadrach, Meshach and Abednego. Were they filled with fear and terror of what awaited them? Would they bow down under pressure? Or did they know who their God was?

With determination, great courage and boldness they said, "Your Majesty, we will not try to defend ourselves. If the God whom we serve is able to save us from the blazing furnace and from your power, then he will. But even if he doesn't Your Majesty you may be sure that we will not worship your god, and we will not bow down to the golden statue that you have set up."

There was a deathly silence in the courtyard, as every eye was on the King to see what would happen next. After hearing that, King Nebuchadnezzar lost his temper, he was seething with anger how dare anybody disobey his instructions, and even more so his senior officials whom he trusted!

He ordered the furnace to be heated seven times hotter than usual, and commanded the strongest men in his army to tie the men up and throw them into the blazing furnace.

The men were dressed in their traditional long robes and had turbines on their heads. They were tied up with thick ropes so that they wouldn't be able to move and were thrown into the blazing furnace.

Now because the king had given strict orders for the furnace to be made extremely hot, as the door was opened, the flames leapt out and killed a couple of the guards who were trying to throw the men into the furnace! Finally, Shadrach, Meshach, and Abednego were thrown into the heart of the blazing fire and the door was firmly closed behind them.

12 FAVOURITE BIBLE STORIES

King Nebuchadnezzar sat on his throne, and watched with glee as they were thrown into the furnace! With that his anger began to subside as he said to himself that nobody would disobey him and get away with it.

As he was staring into the flames, he suddenly jumped up as he thought he was seeing things! Was he going mad? He suddenly saw four people walking around in the flames, and they weren't being burnt up either! In fact he thought the fourth person looked like an angel!

King Nebuchadnezzar rubbed his eyes, and quickly called for one of his officials and asked him "Didn't we tie up three men and throw them into the blazing furnace?" The official assured the King that three men were put into the furnace. The King told his officials that he could see four men walking around! All the senior officials gathered around and everyone was staring into the fire.

King Nebuchadnezzar went up to the door of the blazing furnace stunned and shouted out, "Shadrach! Meshach! Abednego! Servants of the Supreme God! Come out!" With that, the door opened and they stepped out of the furnace. All the King's officials gathered around to look at the three men. They came out completely unharmed, their clothes and hair weren't burnt and they didn't even smell of smoke!

The king shouted out praise to their God who had sent an angel to rescue them! King Nebuchadnezzar immediately promoted them to even higher positions in the province of Babylon than they had before!

DANIEL

Whilst Daniel was in the king's service, King Nebuchadnezzar had several dreams and asked Daniel to interpret them for him. Daniel amongst all the wise men of Babylon was the only one who was given the ability to interpret the dreams correctly.

Over time, King Nebuchadnezzar became proud, cruel and stubborn. His ways became very wicked as he tried to make himself like "a god".

God often speaks to us in dreams and visions when he is trying to say something and get our attention which could be a warning.

God was trying to speak to and warn King Nebuchadnezzar, but he wasn't listening and then God had to intervene and remove him from his position.

The last dream King Nebuchadnezzar had made him very worried. He summoned Daniel to explain the dream to him.

Daniel explained to him, that his royal power was being taken away from him. He would be driven away from his palace, and would live with the wild animals, and eat grass like an ox for seven years, until he acknowledged the power and authority of the one true God.

That day King Nebuchadnezzar was driven from his Palace and became like an animal eating grass. The good news is that after the seven years, he came to his senses and acknowledged the God of Israel and his sanity returned.

Belteshazzar took over from his father Nebuchadnezzar as King of Babylon. He was a bad King, and brought dishonour to God's name just like his father had done. He acted against the Lord and did things his way.

One night there was a large party at the Palace and Belteshazzar was enjoying himself. Suddenly he saw a hand appear on the wall with some writing on it. He became very agitated and wondered if he was seeing things! Daniel was summoned in to interpret the hand writing.

This was another warning sign! Daniel told Belteshazzar that God had numbered the days of his kingdom and had brought it to an end; he had been weighed on the scales; and his kingdom would be divided up and given to the Medes and Persians. That very night Belteshazzar, the king of Babylon was killed.

That same night a man called Darius became the King of Persia, as Babylon fell to the Persians, the Jews now had a new master over them. Daniel was quickly recognized as a very special man and he had favour with the new King.

Dairus the King of Persia valued Daniel's wisdom and skills very much and wanted to put him in charge of the whole empire.

This caused many of those in authority to become jealous of Daniel. They looked for ways to trip him up and find fault with his character but they could not find anything. Daniel was reliable, honest and trustworthy. This made the other officials even more jealous!

One day they got together, to discuss what they could do to get rid of Daniel and hopefully killed!

They decided to hatch up a plan to cause lots of trouble for Daniel. They made an appointment and went to the King, asking him to write out an order, which stated that - for thirty days no one should be allowed to request anything from any god but only to bow down to the King. Anyone who violates this order is to be thrown into a pit filled with lions.

King Darius agreed to this and thought it was a great idea, and signed the order which meant it could never be changed!

When Daniel heard this news, because his faith was so strong in His God, he became defiant and decided that nothing would stop him from doing what he did every day.

Daniel went home as usual and climbed up the stairs to his room. He opened the windows as wide as they would go. Facing towards

Jerusalem he knelt down at the open windows and prayed to his God three times a day.

Daniel's enemies were delighted as their plan was working! They and many others had seen Daniel praying, so they went to the King and reported what they had heard and seen. This was the opportunity they had been waiting for! They told the King that Daniel does not respect your orders and is praying three times a day to his God.

The King valued Daniel very much, and was distressed because he knew he couldn't go back on his order but he wanted to protect Daniel. He wanted to rescue him, but realised that it was no good, as Daniel's enemies wanted to get rid of him and by signing the order he had agreed to this too! The King's word could not be changed.

So finally, he agreed to Daniel being thrown into the pit filled with lions, and he hoped that Daniel's God would rescue him! How he regretted signing that order!

Daniel was grabbed and taken to the edge of a huge pit. Down below were lots of large very hungry lions looking up, licking their lips and waiting for their next meal!

Daniel was pushed hard over the edge and went hurtling down to the bottom of the pit. He landed with a thud amongst the lions. The lions came up to him, sniffed him and then wandered off and lay down at the far end of the pit and went to sleep. A large stone was put across the mouth of the pit and Daniel was left with the lions for the night.

Once the stone had been put over the mouth of the pit, everyone crowded round listening but all was quiet. What was happening? Had he already been torn to pieces?

King Darius went back to his Palace that night very disturbed and he didn't sleep the whole night. He paced up and down in his room all night. He didn't want anything to eat! He was very worried and upset about what he had allowed to be done to Daniel.

The next morning, the king got up very early and rushed over to the pit. He shouted out to Daniel and asked if the God he served had saved him from the lions?

He waited anxiously, and immediately Daniel called out, "Yes! All is well! God sent an angel to shut the mouths of the lions so that they would not hurt me."

The king was so relieved and overjoyed! Daniel was immediately pulled up out of the pit. As they pulled him up there was not a mark on his body. He hadn't been hurt at all because he trusted God with all his heart, and knew that the God of Israel would protect him.

As the King thought about what had been done to Daniel, he became outraged and demanded that all those who had accused Daniel, together with their families be thrown into the pit filled with lions. Before they even reached the bottom of the pit the lions had pounced on them and torn them to pieces.

The news of what happened to Daniel in the lion's den spread all over the Babylonian Empire.

Daniel's God the God of Israel had sent an angel to close the mouths of the lions and saved his life. King Darius issued an order that everyone in his Empire was to serve Daniel's God the God of Israel.

Daniel became even more powerful in the King's Palace. Whatever Daniel put his hand to do God blessed him.

The End

7

THE MIRACLE JAR OF OIL

I grew up in the picturesque village of Joppa which is a fishing village along the Mediterranean coast.

My father was a fisherman, as most men were who lived in that area. Fishing guaranteed a good and regular income. My mother had a large family to look after. I was the eldest and expected to help look after my younger brothers and sisters.

Jewish girls get married very young in our custom. My parents arranged my marriage and I was married when I was 16 years old. As soon as I got married my husband took me away from all my family to live near Nazareth where he worked.

I now live in a small village called Cana in the Galilee, with my husband Levi and our two young sons Noah and Joshua. The nearest big town is Nazareth which is about a two hour walk away. I have lived in the village for about fifteen years.

At first I missed my family very much especially my brothers and sisters. I have seen my family about twice in fifteen years, as Joppa is a couple of days walk away, or it may be a little quicker by donkey, but as we didn't have a donkey it would mean walking.

Life has been lonely at times and it has taken me awhile to make new friends and feel part of village life. My two sons were born in Cana so that helped me, feel part of the community. They go to the village school and we all attend the Synagogue every Friday night. Most of their friends are from the village or the surrounding areas.

My husband Levi was away most of the week as he lived in Nazareth, where there are more job opportunities. He was a builder and worked in the family business. Nazareth was expanding, so a lot of new houses and dwelling places were being built.

However, we are a small closely knit village, and as I have no other extended family they have become my family. If ever we are in trouble or need something, we all help each other, and are there for each other in the good times and hard times.

The water pump is the centre of village life, where we go down to draw water, wash the clothes and gather to chat and discuss our families, village affairs and whatever else is of interest!

The Synagogue also plays a big part in our lives. The whole village attends every Shabbat and all the Feasts and Festivals, weddings and funerals.

I remember, a very special occasion when my eldest son Noah had his "barmitzvah". This is a ceremony for a Jewish boy who has reached the age of 13, and is now ready to observe religious ways, and is eligible to take part in public worship at the synagogue. He can also now read portions from the Torah in the Synagogue.

It was a very exciting day and we had a big party for him, everybody turned out to celebrate the occasion. We had a whole sheep on a bb-q, and lots of the families brought food so it was a great celebration with the whole village involved.

Levi my husband came home every Friday in time for Shabbat, which starts at sunset on Friday and finishes at sunset on Saturday. Shabbat is a special time for Jewish families. It is a time when we sit down and have a meal altogether as a family. My sons love hearing their father read in Hebrew from the Torah (which consists of the first five books of the Old Testament). Nobody works, cooks or cleans on Shabbat. It is a day of rest and a time for families to be together and have fun.

My life is busy in my home, bringing up the children, washing the clothes, cooking, baking bread and cleaning the house.

We are a poor family, my husband works hard but doesn't bring back much money each week for me to be able to feed and clothe my family properly.

I decided one day, to take in washing from other families, which helps me to earn a bit of extra cash.

I had a plan in mind and wanted to save enough money to achieve my goal. So I decided that I was going to save the "washing money" each week, so I hid it away under my mattress.

After a long time of saving, I managed to fulfil my goal which was to buy a goat!

One day, I set off for the market very excited, as today was the day I was going to purchase my goat. I had to walk for an hour to the local market, where they sold sheep, goats and chickens. A few hours later, I came home proudly leading my goat along the road. I had also bought a bell to put around her neck so that I would hear her if she wandered off too far.

All the villagers came out to have a look at her – she was the talk of the village! Every morning and evening, I would go out to the little shed and milk her, she provided enough milk every day for my family and I even managed to sell some.

I also purchased a small piece of land which enabled me to start growing some corn. A neighbour sold me a couple of chickens which gives us a few eggs each day. We were at last beginning to become more self-sufficient.

There are lots of olive trees around where we live, and during the olive season I pick baskets of black and green olives.

My husband made me a small olive press out of blocks of wood, so I was able to press the olives in order to collect the olive oil.

Olive oil is very important to us as we use it for cooking, heating and filling the oil lamps each evening. The olive crop is normally very bountiful, so everyone can enjoy them. Once I have pressed my olives I store the oil in jars. Olives are a great part of our diet as well.

Life was just beginning to become a little easier! I woke up one particular morning, the sun was shining and my children had gone off to school. I was singing as I swept the house, when I heard someone calling my name loudly.

I rushed outside and saw a couple of men running towards me. I just knew it was not good news! My heart was beating very fast! They stopped in front of my house, and told me, that there had been a bad accident where my husband was working. He was working on the roof of a building and had slipped and fallen.

I was shocked and just couldn't believe it and didn't know what I was going to say to my children! It was a very difficult and hard time for the three of us. Life as a widow was very hard and one could be made to feel an outcast.

My sons found it difficult as they missed their father very much. The villagers gathered around us and were very kind. Everyone tried to help us as much as possible.

As time went by, and because there was very little money coming in, I couldn't afford to pay the rent for the little house where we lived! I had to sell our small piece of land in order to pay for the rent and food.

I also became very worried, as I was beginning to have visits from people my husband worked with. They had lent him money and were

THE MIRACLE JAR OF OIL

demanding that they wanted their money paid back to them immediately. My husband had been borrowing money and had run up a very big debt!

I didn't know anything about him borrowing large sums of money. He never told me that he was doing this, and I didn't know how I was going to pay it all back.

My landlord was a hard man and was demanding his rent every month. I told him about our situation, but he wasn't interested as all he wanted was his rent money!

Things were becoming very difficult! I would go without meals so that my children could eat. I began selling the few little bits of furniture that we had. Finally I had to sell my goat, I loved her and she had provided us with milk for a long time and it was also a source of income!

The landlord kept coming to my house, and threatened to take it away, and also take my children as his slaves, in payment for the debts that I now had. (In those days, a landlord had a right to repossess property and even take your children as payment if a family could not pay the bills).

I was desperate, we had no more food in the house, everything had been sold there was nothing left! All I had was a small jar of oil so that we could light the oil lamps at night. I was becoming ill with worry and no food. I didn't know what to do or where to go to for help! I felt hopeless and helpless! I was worried what was going to happen to my sons.

Noah and Jonah found it difficult at school to see their friends with new toys and clothes and they had nothing. At times they had to go to school hungry because we couldn't afford to eat. Our friends tried to help us when they could, but everyone had big families of their own to look after.

I was down at the well as usual one morning, to draw water, and as I was pouring the water into my earthen ware jar, the women were discussing that a Prophet was coming to Cana. They said he was a wonderful man and his name was Elisha.

As I walked slowly back up the hill towards my house, I wondered if he could help me, maybe he was my answer! I had tried to pray to the God of Israel. I didn't know what to do!

We all knew about the Prophet Elijah and the miracles he had done, but people said that the Prophet Elisha was even more famous than Elijah. I thought to myself, I have got nothing to lose I must try and find him. Desperation and urgency pushed me on to find out where Elisha was staying.

Eventually I found him and I didn't care, I pushed my way through the crowd and threw myself at his feet. I sobbed and told him my story! How little by little I had sold my piece of land, the goat, all the furniture and valuables in my home until nothing remained but my two boys.

He took me by the hand and helped me to my feet. He looked at me very kindly, and asked me "What do you have in your house?" I told him I had nothing, and then I remembered that I had a small jar of oil which we used to light the lamps at night.

The Prophet Elisha told me, that I should collect as many empty jars as possible from my neighbours. Bring them home, close the door, and pour the oil from my little jar into the empty containers!

I decided to believe the Prophet Elisha and do what he told me to do. Things couldn't get any worse!

I was so excited, I rushed home and told my sons, to go to every home in the neighbouring villages, and collect jars of all shapes and sizes and bring them back to me.

They came back with lots of different jars of every size and shape! There were clay jars, ceramic ones, bottles and cans. The neighbours also called by with spare jars. My sons kept coming back with more and more jars until they said there weren't any more spare jars to be found anywhere!

I began to pour the oil into the jars as the Prophet had instructed me to do! I poured and poured, filling jar after jar and the most amazing miracle was happening, the oil in my little jar continued to flow out until all the jars in the house were filled! As soon as I had no more jars to fill guess what the oil stopped flowing!

I stood back clapping my hands in amazement! There before us were row upon row of jars filled with pure olive oil. Noah and Jonah looked at all the jars wide eyed, they were wondering how this miracle happened!

THE MIRACLE JAR OF OIL

One small jar of oil had filled dozens and dozens of jars with oil! It was a miracle!

I looked at all the jars and wondered what I should do next? I decided to run back to where the Prophet was staying, and told him what had happened. I asked him, "What shall we do now?" He told me, "Sell the oil and pay off your debt." He told me that there would be more than enough to live off for the rest of our lives for me and my sons!

We left the place where the Prophet Elisha was staying and did exactly what he told us to do.

We went out and sold the jars of oil. People were queueing outside my house to buy the oil. We also sold them in the markets, and before long all the jars of oil had been sold. I collected the money, and as I counted it out, there was more than enough to pay off my very large debt and there was lots of money left over for me and my family.

Everyone was talking about the miracle of the jars of oil! The story went all around the neighbouring villages of the Galilee. When my sons went to school the next day, all their friends crowded around them wanting to know what had happened!

I thanked and praised the God of Israel for the miracle He had done for me and my sons. How He had turned my hopelessness and despair into hope and joy. He had saved my life and also the lives of my sons.

The little I had in my hand was multiplied beyond my wildest dreams.

The End

8

MARTHA & MARY

I live with my sister Mary and brother Lazarus in Bethany. The little village of Bethany is about 2 miles outside of Jerusalem, and located on the south-eastern slope of the Mount of Olives. Today, Bethany is a small village known as e-Azariyeh, meaning place of Lazarus.

We know everyone in the village as we have been born in Bethany and have lived here all our lives. Our house is always full of visitors it seems to be the centre of the village where people congregate.

I love it but sometimes all I seem to do is cook, bake bread, wash and sweep the house! Jesus and His twelve disciples are regular visitors to our home. We love it when Jesus comes to stay and the best times are when Jesus comes either on His own or with three of His special disciples Peter, James and John. Jesus is our best friend in the whole world.

When I know Jesus is on his way to come and visit us, I am rushing around the house to make sure that everything is just right! I am cooking and baking special foods which I know he will love.

It is a wonderful privilege and honour to have Jesus to stay, and the fact that He wants to come and stay with us in our home. As soon as Jesus arrives He greets us with a Hebrew word "Shalom"! Shalom means peace and that is just what happens, suddenly a peace descends on our home, and all the stress and frustrations seem to disappear.

Jesus doesn't have His own home and He travels around with His disciples all over Israel. Whenever Jesus was tired, and needed a break from the crowds He would come and stay. He told us that He always felt so "at home" and welcomed. We kept a special room which was always waiting for him, as we never knew when He was coming.

The only problem is that when people know that Jesus is staying with us, everyone wants to see Him!

Men, women and children pour into our home to be able to be near Him. He is a wonderful teacher and tells us stories, in a way that we can understand what he is saying. There are many people in our village and the surrounding villages who are blind, lame, deaf and troubled by different things, and they all want to be touched and healed by Jesus.

Often times, I am exhausted when He arrives with all the preparations, as I want things to be perfect for Him. We don't have fridges and freezers, and because it is so hot in Israel, food has to be prepared and eaten the same day. Sometimes I feel that I am the only one doing any work in preparing for the visitors! When there is work to do suddenly, my brother and sister seem to disappear or are very busy doing something else!

I remember one particular occasion, Jesus and His twelve disciples were coming to stay!

There was so much to do and how was I going to get it all done. The house needed to be cleaned, water fetched from the well (I had hoped Lazarus would offer to do that!), meals prepared and lots of other jobs.

I was adding up how many meals would need to be prepared; how many loaves of bread needed to be baked and to make matters worse, they would all be staying during Shabbat! Shabbat starts from sunset on Friday evening until sunset on Saturday. In our Jewish custom nobody is allowed to cook or prepare food over Shabbat, so everything has to be prepared ahead of time.

Jesus and His disciples arrived and it was wonderful to see them! I was rushing around! Mary and Lazarus welcomed them in.

Jesus sat down on His favourite recliner chair and my sister Mary, immediately sat down at Jesus feet looking up at Him. Jesus started talking, and Mary wanted to hear and listen to every word he had to say. Mary really loved Jesus so much! I rather envied the way Mary loved Jesus and she just longed to be with Him all the time. I loved Him too but I never seemed to have enough time to spend with Him, because I was always in the kitchen working.

It was midday I was busy preparing the food in the kitchen and could hear Jesus talking with the others. I wanted so much to be there too, but if I didn't prepare the food we wouldn't have anything to eat!

As I thought about things, I was feeling very sorry for myself, and getting crosser and crosser that no one was helping me. I began to bang a few pots around in the hopes that Mary would get the message and come and help! No joy there!

I could stand it no longer, and burst into the room, interrupting Jesus I'm afraid, and I asked, "Lord, do you not care that my sister has left me to do all the work by myself? Tell her to help me." I gave Mary a good long stare!

Jesus looked at me very lovingly and kindly, and called me over to where He was sitting. In a gentle rebuke He said, "Martha, Martha, you are worried about so many things; but there is only one thing that is important and lasting and that is spending time with Me. Mary has chosen the best part to sit with Me."

I was upset and felt disappointed with myself, but I realised that He was right! I was so busy doing things but to be with Jesus and spend time with Him was so much better.

I love Jesus very much and I wanted to love Him more and learn from Mary, that to be with Jesus was the most important thing in life.

After some time, our brother Lazarus suddenly became seriously ill. We were worried and upset and sent a message to Jesus to come to us immediately.

Jesus also loved Lazarus very much. He took such a long time in coming, however, after a few days my brother died. We buried him in a tomb which was like a cave.

We were so upset that our brother was no longer with us. The whole village came to comfort us. Everyone loved Lazarus and the villagers were as shocked as we were! Where was Jesus? Why hadn't He come? Did He not care?

A few days later, I heard that Jesus had arrived and was on the outskirts of Bethany. I ran all the way to where He was and told Jesus that if had been here, my brother would not have died! Jesus told me, that everything was going to be alright and that my brother was only asleep!

I didn't understand what He was saying, as we all knew that Lazarus had died!

I walked slowly, back to the house and called Mary, and told her privately, that Jesus is here and is calling for you. Mary jumped up and ran out to where Jesus was she knelt at His feet and also told the Lord, if you had been here, my brother would not have died.

Jesus asked us where Lazarus was. We took Him to the tomb, by this time all our visitors had joined us too. Jesus demanded that we took away the big heavy stone which had been rolled in front of the tomb. We were shocked because Lazarus had been dead for a few days now! Jesus had spoken and everyone obeyed and we all helped to roll the stone back. Jesus told us if we believed we would see the glory of God! We wondered what that meant! Everyone was quiet and all eyes were fixed on Jesus!

I will always remember the amazing confident prayer Jesus prayed. He looked up towards heaven and said, "Father, I thank you for having heard me. I know that you always hear me, but I have said this for the sake of the crowd standing here, so that they may believe that you sent me."

He suddenly shouted out very loudly, "Lazarus, come out!"

There was shocked silence! The air was filled with expectancy beyond our wildest dreams! Nobody moved or said a word! We waited for what seemed like forever, but in fact it was only a matter of seconds, when suddenly, we heard a sound coming from inside the cave, there was a rustling and some movement, and then … Lazarus came out! His hands and feet were bound up with strips of cloth, and his head was also wrapped in a cloth. We stood still in shock and amazement, every emotion was running high! Jesus told us to take off all the strips of cloths which were bound round him.

You can imagine the screams of delight at having our brother back with us. It seemed like we were in a dream, it was too good to be true! There was much celebration and we had a special meal with Lazarus, Jesus and His disciples.

Whenever Jesus came to visit us, He explained more to us about who He is and the Kingdom He has come from and in time going back to. We didn't understand a lot of what He told us - we had so many questions.

Then Jesus began to tell us some very sad news, that soon He wouldn't be able to visit us at Bethany as He was going away!

We wondered where He was going to? We couldn't bear to think what our lives would be like without Him. The thought of Him not visiting us and staying the night was almost unthinkable. How would His disciples feel, as they had been with Jesus for nearly three years.

It had been a little while since Jesus, had visited us, in fact He hadn't been back since Lazarus was raised from the dead. It was a few days before Passover, which is a special festival that all Jewish people celebrate.

Passover (Pesach in Hebrew) takes place in the spring time, and commemorates the deliverance of us the Jewish people from captivity in Egypt, and when we left Egypt and passed through the Red Sea.

We heard that Jesus was coming back to Bethany, with all of His disciples, so we decided to lay on a special dinner for them. I served everyone as usual and after we had eaten the meal we were sitting around talking and enjoying each other's company.

Mary suddenly got up and disappeared for a while, and I wondered where she had gone to. On her return I noticed that she had her beautiful alabaster jar in her arms which was filled with a very expensive perfume. She had been given this alabaster jar, several years before and it was very special to her.

Alabaster jars were often made from a precious stone found in Israel. This stone resembles the texture of marble, and was extremely expensive to own. These jars contained ointments, oils and perfume. The thick stone prevented the aroma from escaping and kept the perfume from spoiling. The shape of the jar usually had a long neck and a sealed top. In order to open the jar, the top had to be broken, which allowed it to be used only once.

Mary went over and sat at Jesus feet, which was her favourite position. As she broke open the jar, the whole house was filled with the fragrance of the perfume. She started anointing Jesus' feet with the perfume, and as she untied her beautiful long brown hair she wiped Jesus' feet with her hair.

We were rather shocked and amazed wondering what would happen next. I knew that this was a way of Mary expressing her deep love for Jesus. The noise died down in the house, as every eye was on Mary and then we waited for Jesus' reaction.

Judas Iscariot, one of His disciples (the one who was going to betray Him) was the first to speak. He was very cross and asked why this perfume was not being sold and the money given to the poor? Judas didn't really care about poor people at all, but would rather have kept the money for himself as he was very greedy.

Jesus told Judas, "Leave her alone. She bought it so that she might keep it for the day of my burial. You will always have the poor with you, but you will not always have me."

12 FAVOURITE BIBLE STORIES

It was soon after this that our beloved Rabbi and friend Jesus, was arrested and put on a cross to die. Our Jewish leaders were very jealous of Jesus and just wanted to get rid of Him, as He challenged them and they didn't like that at all. Jesus told us that He was willing to die, so that all of us can have our sins forgiven and be with God His Father forever.

We followed Jesus right to the end of His life. We missed Him so much but the story doesn't end there because He told us that He was going to rise again from the dead after three days.

That is exactly what happened! Mary was one of the first people to see Jesus in a garden after He had risen from the dead.

Our hearts were filled with such joy and happiness!

The End

9

JAIRUS'S LITTLE DAUGHTER

It was early in the morning, and a boat had just arrived at the port of Tiberias. A very large crowd had already gathered by the edge of the Sea of Galilee waiting for Jesus. Tiberias is the main city in the Galilee, and it is a bustling fishing port. People were pushing and shoving trying to get close to Jesus and His disciples as they climbed out of their boat.

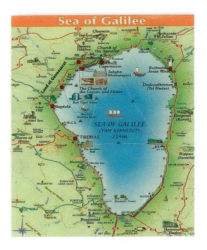

There was great jubilation and excitement from the crowd, as Jesus and His disciples joined them. Jesus was talking to His disciples when suddenly there was a disturbance in the crowd.

One of the well-known Synagogue leaders called Jairus, started calling out loudly to Jesus, pushing and elbowing his way through the crowd. He had such a look of fear and anguish on his face. He was desperate to get to Jesus, but the crowd was so large, he had to push his way against the flow of people to get to Jesus.

Jairus was a rabbi at the local Synagogue and everybody in the town knew him.

Finally, when he got to Jesus he fell down at His feet and sobbed. His little daughter, who was only twelve years of age, was at home very sick! He wanted Jesus to come NOW and put His hands on her, because he knew that just one touch from Jesus his little daughter would be healed. Jesus looked at him lovingly and nodded.

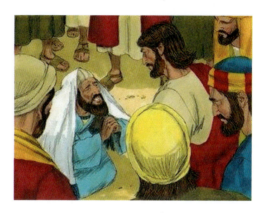

Jairus knew of many people who had been healed by Jesus, and he knew that by Jesus coming to his house was all that it would take for a miracle to happen for his little girl. Jairus only had one daughter and he was so fearful that she would die.

Oh! How he wished Jesus would move along faster, time was passing by, he needed to get him to his daughter now! However, Jesus was not in a hurry! There was such a large crowd pressing against Him and His disciples, which made walking fast impossible! Jesus was available for everyone, and would never pass anyone by who needed Him.

Poor Jairus was so frustrated, and couldn't understand why Jesus wasn't making his desperate situation a priority! His daughter could easily die, who knows she might have already died!

Suddenly, to make matters worse, someone saw a woman crouching down and pushing her way through the crowd trying to get to Jesus.

She was a little frail woman who looked very frightened. It turned out she didn't want to speak to Jesus, she only wanted to touch the tassel on the edge of His robe that was all she wanted to do. She didn't want to disturb Him, as she knew He would have more important things to do.

It had taken all the courage she had to come out into the town, but she heard that Jesus was around, and knew that her only hope was to touch Him. She was very poor as she had spent all her money on treatment from doctors and nothing had helped her, in fact she was getting worse and worse as the days went by.

She often felt like an outcast and had no friends or family, and because of her illness, she very rarely left her house and was all alone in the world.

So this particular morning, she knew that this was her moment, Jesus was passing through Tiberias, and she might not have another opportunity again.

She got dressed and decided she would have to go out into the town. She put a shawl over her head and covered most of her face so that no one would recognise her. She was following at quite a distance from the rest of the crowd, and trying to figure out how she could get close enough to Jesus. Eventually, she saw a small gap in the crowd, and crouching down she worked her way through and suddenly, she saw the tassels on the edge of His robe moving, and thought to herself, if I can just reach out, and touch them and then get away again as quickly as possible!

Here was her moment, she reached out and touched the tassel! Instantly she could feel a power go through her body and she knew that she had been healed! Immediately, Jesus stopped and looked around and asked one of His disciples, "Who touched Me?" Everyone was pressing against Jesus but He knew that someone had specifically touched Him, as He felt power leave his body.

She knew it was all over, now she would have to own up that she had touched Him! The crowd made room for her and trembling all over she came to Jesus and knelt down and told Him everything.

Jesus looked at her with such love and said to her, "Daughter, your faith has healed you." Immediately, she stood up no longer crouching and ashamed! She went on her way happy and healed.

Jairus was delighted for the lady, but was wondering how long before his miracle would happen. He was very worried as so much time had passed now, and they were still quite away from his house.

As Jesus and the crowd starting walking again, suddenly, a servant from Jairus's house came running up to Jairus, and told him that his daughter had died, and not to bother Jesus anymore as there was no need.

Jesus overheard this and looked straight at Jairus and told him, "Do not be afraid! Just believe." Jairus loved and trusted Jesus and believed that He could do anything, but this was the worst news possible!

Jairus had to make a decision to either believe the news from his servant, or to believe Jesus and not to fear!

By this time, they were nearing his house, and they could hear all the relatives crying.

Jesus walked away from the crowds, and went into Jairus's house, with three of His special disciples Peter, James and John. Jesus told all the relatives to stop crying as the little girl was asleep! They lifted up their heads and laughed mockingly at Jesus!

Jesus then took the little girl's mother and father, His three disciples and went into the room where the little girl was lying and closed the door.

Her parents crowded round the bed, and in spite of their shock and sadness there was an air of expectancy.

Jesus was in the room and there was such a peace and calm! Everyone in the room believed that she was going to wake up! Jesus walked over to her took her by the hand, and in Aramaic the local language said, "Talitha koum!" which means, "Little girl, Get Up!"

Immediately she sat up and gave Jesus and her parents a big hug. There was so much joy and happiness in the room. Their little girl had been given back to them.

JAIRUS'S LITTLE DAUGHTER

As she got up and ran out of the room, there was a stunned silence, as all the relatives and the other disciples, watched her skipping out of the house into the garden to play.

That day, one lady went home healed, full of joy and hope and a family were rejoicing over their little girl who had died and was now alive!

The End

10

ZACCHAEUS THE TAX COLLECTOR

& BLIND BARTIMAEUS

I was one of Jesus disciples and had travelled around with him and the others for nearly three years. They were the best years of my life. We had learnt so much being with Jesus and had seen Him perform the most amazing miracles.

I loved it when Jesus suggested we went up into the hills with him for a while to get away from the crowds. Sometimes we went to stay with Martha and Mary in Bethany. He would teach us about the Kingdom of God and many other things. He often spoke in parables, which were stories so that we would understand what he was saying. We were quite a motley crew of disciples! Most of us were big burley fishermen and there was also Matthew who was a tax collector.

There were three of us who were the closest to Jesus –Simon Peter was the outspoken one, John was a special friend of Jesus and then me James. John and I were brothers. The three of us, experienced things with Jesus that some of the others never did. Just recently, Jesus started telling us about all the things that were going to happen to Him. He was going to suffer at the hands of the religious leaders, and He would be killed and then later be raised from the dead. We couldn't get our heads around this. We knew the religious leaders hated Him, but how could that be, Jesus our dearest friend, with whom we had lived with for 3 years.

ZACCHAEUS THE TAX COLLECTOR & BLIND BARTIMAEUS

I remember one day, Jesus took the three of us, Simon Peter, John and me, up a very high mountain.

All of a sudden a thick mist came down and we could see Jesus changing before our eyes. His face shone like the sun and His clothes became like a very bright white light.

We were terrified and couldn't look at Him because of the brilliant light which shone all around Him. It was as though there were shafts of glory all around us. We turned around and suddenly, Moses and Elijah also joined us on the mountain and were talking to Jesus.

All of a sudden a bright cloud covered them and we heard a voice coming out of the clouds, "This is my Son, whom I love; I am well pleased with Him. Listen to Him!" We were quite shaken up and filled with wonder and amazement after this experience. Jesus told us not to say a word about what happened until after He had risen from the dead.

We used to talk about this experience often when we were on our own and we will never be the same again as a result.

We travelled all over the Galilee and other places with Jesus. On one occasion, we had just arrived in the village of Jericho. A crowd was gathering and people were calling out to Jesus, as we walked along the road. The three of us Peter, John and I always stayed close to Jesus as He walked amongst the crowd, and the other disciples mingled amongst the rest of the crowd.

We were walking under the shade of some sycamore-fig trees which were lining the street. When Jesus suddenly stopped and looked up into the tree! We all stopped wondering what He was looking at! No one had seen a little man run ahead and climb up a tree so that he could have a bird's eye view of Jesus! We stood open mouthed as Jesus called out and said to him, "Zacchaeus, come down immediately. I must come to your house today." How did He know his name? Jesus never ceased to amaze us!

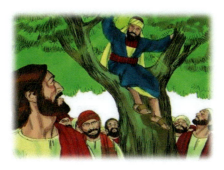

Zacchaeus was a very unpopular man in Jericho no one liked him or wanted to be his friend. He was the chief tax collector and very wealthy. The reason he was so wealthy, was because he robbed people by charging them high amounts of taxes which he happily collected from them! Zacchaeus was very short and people laughed at him and made fun of him and it made him feel very lonely!

The people in the crowd were grumbling and not happy that Jesus was going to be a friend of this greedy man, who robbed them and made their lives miserable! They couldn't understand why Jesus was going to have a meal with this horrible little man!

As soon as Jesus called Zacchaeus, he jumped down from the tree so fast and looked so happy and excited. He took Jesus and all of us disciples to his house, and gave us a delicious meal.

After the meal, Zacchaeus started to tell Jesus how he had cheated people, and that he was so sorry and wanted to give half of his possessions to the poor, and he will even pay back four times the amount of money he has taken from people!

The amazing thing is Jesus never condemned him or even said a word about him being a greedy tax collector, but he felt convicted just by being in Jesus Presence.

That day a new life of hope and generosity started for Zaachaeus. Where before he was hated and had no friends, suddenly as he became generous and kind everybody wanted to be his friend! He had never had so many invitations to come into people's houses for a meal.

Just one encounter with Jesus changed everything for Zaachaeus!

It had been a long day, crowds and crowds of people were still following Jesus.

It was late in the afternoon, and we were just leaving Jericho, after having spent time with Zaachaeus. We were hot and tired as we walked along the dusty road. I noticed a beggar man sitting on the side of the road in the hot sun. He had been there for hours waiting for Jesus to pass by.

He was blind and wasn't able to follow the crowd. The only reason he knew that Jesus was near was because of all the shouting of the crowd. He was desperate for Jesus to touch him! He had heard that He healed people. He started shouting out loudly for Jesus. He had been born blind and all he wanted to do was to be able to see. He had never seen a sunrise or a sunset!

The only way he could live was to beg. He went to the same place in the village each day, and put his begging bowl out in front of him, hoping that someone would be generous and throw in a shekel or two! Someone might even give him some bread, if it was a really good day! Bartimaeus was desperate as he was sick of his way of life! There had to be a better way!

The crowd was beginning to move on and he started shouting with all his might, "Jesus, Son of David, help me! Jesus, Son of David, help me!" The people in the crowd told him to shut up and be quiet! The more people told him to be quiet, this made Bartimaeus call out all the louder, "Jesus, Son of David, help me!"

Jesus immediately stopped, and looked over at Bartimaeus and told him to come over to Him. A couple of people standing near-by told him, quick get up Jesus is calling for you to come to Him.

Bartimaeus jumped up, threw off his ragged old coat, left his bowl behind which had a few coins in it, and ran in the direction of Jesus voice. A couple of people standing nearby brought him right up to Jesus.

Jesus asked him, "What do you want me to do for you?" I was always amazed when Jesus asked that question because He could see Bartimaeus was blind!

Bartimaeus answered, "Master, I want to see!" Jesus told him, "You may go. Your eyes are healed because of your faith." The man gave a loud shriek of delight as his eyes suddenly popped open and he could see! He stood in amazement as he looked all around him, taking in the sights of the crowd for the first time. By this time, the crowd had started moving on and he ran along and joined in following Jesus.

He had already forgotten all about his ragged old coat and his begging bowl! He was leaving his old miserable life behind him and starting a brand new life of hope and joy.

He told everyone he met what Jesus had done for him and that he was no longer blind Bartimaeus but now he could see!

The End

11

A SMALL BOY'S LUNCH

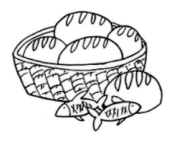

I live with my parents, 6 brothers and 4 sisters in a small village called Capernaum which is on the shores of the Sea of Galilee. The synagogue is the central meeting point of the village. Everybody knows each other and we are a closely knit community.

I am growing up in a Jewish family. I love Shabbat which starts at sunset on Friday evening and it begins with a special meal with the whole family.

My mother lights the candles of the menorah, (which is a special candlestick with 7 candles) and sings a prayer of blessing over us, and then my Father reads from the Torah. Before Shabbat it is a very busy time for my mother, as she prepares all the meals for her large family for the next 24 hours. No housework, cooking or washing up will be done over Shabbat until Saturday sunset.

Meals in a Jewish family are a special time for the family to spend time together. We normally have breakfast and the evening meal all together. My eldest brother, fetches the Torah scrolls down from the cupboard, and gives them to my father who reads a proportion from the Torah at the beginning of everyday. (The Torah is the first five books of the Old Testament).

Our customs are very special to us and part of our way of life on a daily basis.

We celebrate the Jewish Feasts and Festivals, of which there are many. Most of them are a time for celebration.

I have two favourite Festivals which I love. The first one is Purim, which is the story of Queen Esther who saved us the Jewish people from being killed by the evil Haman. This is a joyous time as we celebrate the fact that the wicked Haman's plan didn't succeed. We dress up in fun costumes, play games and are given sweets and other treats.

My second favourite, is the Feast of Tabernacles, and this is a very special festival. We make a booth type house out of leaves and reeds, and we live and eat in this booth for 8 days. This festival is to commemorate the years that the Israelites wandered in the desert after they left Egypt.

It is great fun building our booths. The whole family is involved, we go out into the country side to cut down reeds, grasses and leaves, and come home bearing all our bounty. My father and three of my eldest brothers are in charge of erecting the booth, and then us younger ones help to decorate it inside. Everyone in the village is also out in the country side as they are building their own booths.

It is soon coming up to another one of our important Feasts in the Jewish calendar called Passover.

Passover (Pesach in Hebrew) takes place in the spring time, and commemorates the deliverance of us the Jewish people from captivity in Egypt, and when we left Egypt and passed through the Red Sea.

However, it is very early in the morning, as I lie on my mattress on the floor. All is quiet my mother, brothers and sisters are still asleep. I ponder with excitement, not quite knowing why, except that today is a special day, as there is no school and the whole day lies ahead of me to play with my friends.

After some time, the sun starts peeping up over the Sea of Galilee, casting a silvery path across the waters. The rooster starts giving his usual early morning wake up calls. The goats are getting restless in their pen, waiting to be let out on this beautiful morning.

The whole village is beginning to stir as the day will soon begin. I got up bleary eyed and walked out of our little house. I could see in the distance, the fishermen bringing in their boats with the haul from a night's fishing. My father is a fisherman, and he has been out all night on the Sea of Galilee.

I love watching the boats coming in, the men straining as they pull in the nets is a sight which always gives me a thrill. The fishermen sort out the catch and anything that is no good is discarded to one side, and the rest of the fish is boxed up and later on taken to market. The fishermen sit on the beach, chatting about the night's catch or their family's latest news, as they clean their boats and mend the nets in preparation for the next night's fishing.

My mother calls out to me to get washed and dressed. I walk down to the water pump which is located in the centre of the village, to fetch the water in an earthen ware jar and bring it back to the house. It isn't too far but the water jar is heavy once filled up with water. The water pump is another gathering point in the village, where the clothes are washed, the women fetch the water for their households and they chat and laugh, while the children play nearby.

A SMALL BOY'S LUNCH

I am looking forward to being with my friends today. We are all from the same village and go to the same Synagogue every Shabbat (Saturday). We are planning to be out all day playing on the shores of the Sea of Galilee, and may be trying to do some fishing in the shallows with our rods, which comprises of a stick and a piece of string with a hook on the end.

By the time I got back from the water pump, the fire had been lit, and the kettle filled with sweet mint tea was on the boil and filling the house with a wonderful aroma. Mother is kneading the dough to make loaves of bread for the day's meals. She is also making small olive pitta breads. I love hearing her sing as she kneads the bread and sweeps the house. Later on my Father, whom we call Abba, arrives home, with some fish from the night's fishing. He is tired after a hard night out on the lake, but he always has time for us kids.

I am extra excited today, and sense that something special is going to happen.

I asked my mother if I can have a packed lunch as I am going to be out all day with my friends. I am 8 years old, and my mother only allowed me to go out for the day, if I am with my friends who are a little older than I. She has packed me up five small freshly baked barley loaves of bread and two fresh silvery sardines which she has put in a red spotted handkerchief.

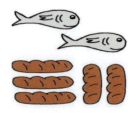

My friends Jacob, Nathaniel, Ariel and I set off with our rods and packed lunches. It is very exciting to be going out for the day, and leaving my brothers and sisters behind at home!

We set off for the shores of the Sea of Galilee and played there for hours, and then decided to move round the Lake, to a neighbouring village called Bethsaida which isn't too far from Capernaum. Bethsaida is a small pretty fishing village, and we have some aunts and uncles who live there.

We have just arrived when, we noticed a crowd gathering and there is a lot of shouting and excitement. Some little boats have arrived on the shore and several men got out. We are wondering what is happening, and asked someone in the crowd.

Why they said, it is Jesus of Nazareth who has come with some of His disciples! I don't know who this Jesus is, but people told me He is a Rabbi – a teacher, a very important person and He heals people of lots of different sicknesses and diseases.

Suddenly, a huge crowd started gathering and everyone was following Jesus and calling out to Him. I thought he must be quite famous, as so many people are following him! I met some of my relatives amongst the crowd and they said, come let's follow Jesus! There was a lot of jostling in the crowd, as everyone wanted to get close to Him.

I managed to get quite close too and I saw him touching people, and they immediately got healed. A man who was lame, he couldn't walk properly Jesus touched Him and he immediately could walk without a limp.

Jesus has a very loving and compassionate look in his eyes as He looks at people. I am so drawn to this man called Jesus that I couldn't stop looking at Him. I wanted Him to touch me even though I wasn't sick!

Jesus and his companions called disciples, were walking towards a large hillside, the crowd by now had grown and grown so large. I don't know how many but there were many, many men, women and children all following and calling out after Jesus.

As I am small, my friends and I got pushed to the back of the crowd, but we elbowed our way in to make sure that we didn't get left behind! We wanted to follow this man called Jesus too.

We scrambled up the grassy bank of the hillside, which was covered in an array of spring flowers. Jesus sat down on a large rock and the little children were running up to Him. He picked them up and put them on His knee, stroked their hair and talked to them I don't know what He was saying to them as I was so far back.

Jesus started telling us stories. He was a wonderful story teller, no one in the crowd moved as they listened to His every word.

I have such a longing and ache in my heart to be one of the children He picks up and puts on His knee. I loved this man called Jesus and I didn't know why, but longed to be close to Him and touch Him.

I suddenly realised that it was getting late in the afternoon as I noticed, the afternoon shadows were lengthening across the hillside. I can only tell the time by the position of the sun, and it was beginning to drop down so I knew it must be getting late.

In the excitement, of all the crowds and following Jesus, I had completely forgotten about my lunch, and suddenly I felt very hungry! I was longing to start eating my fish and barley loaves. Should I start now and eat it quickly?!

Jesus all of sudden stood up and called out, asking the people to sit down on the grass. People sat down in large groups. There was a feeling of great excitement that something was about to happen.

I heard a murmuring going on around me, one of Jesus disciples they called Andrew, started going around and asking if anyone in the crowd had any bread?!

It turned out that Jesus was concerned about the large crowd who must be hungry, as they had had nothing to eat all day and it was getting late. Jesus wanted to feed ALL these people!

Andrew, Jesus disciple, came right up to where I was sitting with my friends, aunts and cousins. I felt that his eyes looked straight into mine! I was sure that he had seen my spotted handkerchief filled with my lunch!

I quickly thought should I hide my lunch!! How would my little lunch feed such a large crowd anyway! It seemed a silly idea to offer it!

I didn't have that thought for too long, as there was such a longing in my heart to give the little that I had to Jesus.

Andrew, by this time had moved away some distance. I quickly got up, picked up my little red spotted handkerchief, which was bulging with the five loaves and two fish, and slightly trembling I went over to Andrew and tugged at his shirt sleeve. He stopped and looked down at me, as I offered him my red spotted handkerchief!

Andrew looked down at me very kindly. I had such a peace in my heart as I gave my lunch to him. I knew if I had kept it I wouldn't have enjoyed it one bit, although it was one of my favourite meals.

He opened up the handkerchief, and called out to Jesus and said, I have 5 loaves and two small fish here, which a little boy has just given to me. A hush came over the crowd again, and Jesus called for the loaves and fish to be brought to Him.

Andrew hurried over and gave my very small offering to Jesus. Jesus then looked up towards heaven and prayed over my loaves and fish.

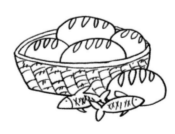

My eyes are out on stalks, as my loaves and fish are being handed out to the crowd of people, as basket after basket is being passed around. Everyone kept eating and eating! The food kept multiplying there is now so much food! Everybody ate till they couldn't eat anymore!

Jesus then asked that all the leftovers were collected up and put into baskets. I couldn't believe it, the disciples counted 12 baskets full of leftovers!

As the crowd began to disperse to go to their various homes and villages, I left with not only a full tummy but a full heart. I had given something so small to Jesus and He had multiplied the little I had until there was more than enough!

I started walking home slowly back to Capernaum. My head was full of all the amazing things I have seen and heard about this man called Jesus. Jesus had used the little I gave him – only 5 loaves and 2 fish and He multiplied it again and again. What would have happened if I hadn't been willing to give him my lunch – how much I would have missed out!

Who is this Jesus? How could I get to know Him? Would I see Him again? I had so many questions and thoughts.

I saw in the distance, the oil lamps twinkling from the different houses in my village. I could see my own house and I ran back home, as fast as I could as I longed to be back with my family.

I hoped I wouldn't be in trouble as I am very late, and anyway, what am I going to say and will they believe me!

My mother scolded me for being late! The table was all set for the evening meal and the family have gathered around the table.

Everybody is talking at the same time, as they talk about what they have been doing that day.

I am very quiet as I was in another world! My father spoke to me, but I never heard him, then all eyes were on me as they wanted to know where I had been!

I began to tell them about this wonderful man called Jesus, how He had healed people, picked up and hugged the little children!

It was very quiet around the meal table my family were enthralled, as I told them about what happened to my five barley loaves and two small sardines!

That night as I looked out at the starry sky, my mind and heart were filled with such joy, peace and happiness!

News has travelled, and the next morning the whole village is buzzing and talking about what had happened the day before.

Everybody now wanted to see Jesus, and we heard that He was still in our area.

As is our custom each Saturday, my father, brothers and I went to the Synagogue in Capernaum. We sat and heard the Torah being read by learned Rabbis, although normally I wasn't too interested and didn't understand much of it!

This particular Saturday, we went as usual to the Synagogue, and to my shock and delight Jesus is there sitting in the crowd! After a while Jesus stood up, there is an awed hush and He began to teach about the Kingdom of God. I am struck again about the Presence that Jesus carries and the love and compassion in His eyes.

He spoke and then sat down, there is a tangible sense of His presence, but some of the learned Rabbis started arguing with Him. Jesus didn't say a word and after a while quietly left the synagogue.

Jesus was staying in Capernaum for a few days, and was invited into one our neighbour's home. Once people heard that He was in our village, they came from near and far, many sick people came to the house wanting to be healed by Jesus until there was no room to move!

We crowded into the house to listen to Jesus, when suddenly there was a rustling and a noise in the roof. Some of the tiles and plaster started falling down! There was a real commotion going on up on the roof! Jesus stopped speaking, and as we looked up, there was a huge hole in the roof!

A man who is unable to walk is being lowered on his mat into the house by some of his friends in front of Jesus. He was desperate to be healed by Jesus!

As the man's friends couldn't get him in through the door of the house because of the crowd, they decided to make another plan and climbed up on to the roof of the house!

You could see the look of delight on Jesus's face because of this man's faith and his desire to be healed! Jesus healed him immediately. The man got up, picked up his mat and walked out of the house in front of everybody! I saw it with my own eyes! There was so much excitement in the house that day as many people were healed.

A couple of years later by then I am about 10 years old, and I hear some very sad news. I am told that Jesus is going to be killed and put on a cross by some cruel men. The leaders of the synagogues are jealous of Jesus and hate Him.

He has never done anything wrong. He healed people and did lots of miracles.

I still remember the miracle with my lunch I gave to Jesus. He has so much love and compassion and only does good things. Jesus is going to die so that we can be forgiven for the wrong and bad things we do and so that we can have peace in our hearts.

Because of what I have seen, heard and believed, I have given Him my love and my heart and have asked Him to come and live inside me.

The End

12

THE NATIVITY

The Inn Keeper

A man called Caesar Augustus issued an order that a census should be taken of the entire Roman world. This was done because the Roman government wanted to make sure that everyone in the Empire were paying their taxes correctly. The census was carried out all over the Empire (most of Europe): but in Israel, it was carried out in a Jewish way rather than a Roman way. This meant that families had to register in their own town rather than where they lived. People had travelled from all over the country, as everyone had to go to their own town to register.

Our Inn in Bethlehem has been so busy the last few days! We are bursting at the seams and are completely full. We just can't squeeze in another person! It has been very good for business!

There has been a steady stream of people arriving for several days now all through the day and night. They are arriving by horse, donkey, camel and on foot. The courtyard is full of animals that need to be put in barns and given food and water. The kitchen's a hive of activity as my wife is busy preparing endless meals.

It is the end of yet another busy day! Finally the Inn is settling down for the night and the last person has checked in. Everybody has been fed and my wife and I are now wearily clearing up and settling down for the night. I was just beginning to put the oil lamps out, when I heard a clipperty clop, clipperty clop of donkey's hooves over the cobbled courtyard.

I listened and waited, and then there was a knock at the door. I opened it and standing there at the door was a man, who asked me anxiously if there was any room in the Inn.

I told him that I was very sorry but I couldn't help him, as there was just no room for them. As I peered into the darkness, I saw a young woman sitting on a donkey. She looked so tired, weary and hungry. I noticed that she was expecting a baby. They had been travelling for several days, probably about 70 miles, from Nazareth to Bethlehem, as they had also come to register.

I was very tired, but my heart went out to this young couple. I thought for a minute, and then told them that all I had was a stable which they would be very welcome to use, but they would have to share it with a few animals!

I quickly fetched a broom and bucket and started sweeping and cleaning the stable as much as I could. I moved the cows and goats up to one end and prepared part of the stable for them to be able to sleep. I gave them some extra blankets, and my wife gave them something to eat. I left the manger full of soft hay for the animals.

There was something special about this couple, and I wanted to do all I could to help them. The young woman was called Mary, she had such a beautiful, contented, peaceful look on her face and her husband Joseph was very caring and loving towards her.

I walked across the courtyard thinking and wondering about them! Little did I know, what was going to happen that night!

In the stillness of the night Mary gave birth to her firstborn, a son. She wrapped him up in cloths and because she had no fancy crib, she placed him in the manger. This was no normal baby! This was the Son of God, the Messiah whom we had all been longing for all our lives!

In the early hours when everyone was fast asleep, there was an arrival of some visitors who had been told about the Baby and had come to see Him!

His birth was inconspicuous, only a humble stable and a manger filled with hay for the Son of God!

The Shepherds

It was a very clear night and the stars were particularly bright and twinkling. Several of us were out in the fields, as usual watching over the sheep in order to keep any predators away.

I loved being out in the fields at night, as there was plenty of time to think! We were huddled round the fire as it can get very chilly at night. All was quiet except for the occasional bleating of the sheep.

It was the early hours of the morning I was just beginning to nod off to sleep! When suddenly, the sky lit up with the most brilliant light I had ever seen. We all jumped up wide eyed, and had to cover our eyes from the brilliance of the light. The brilliant light lit up all the fields around us. There was an expectancy that something was about to happen!

An enormous angel of the Lord suddenly appeared in the sky together with the heavenly hosts! The sky was filled with myriads of angels praising God!

They were saying:

"Glory to God in the highest heaven, and on earth peace to those on whom his favour rests."

We were terrified! This must be a very important announcement! What was happening?

The angel suddenly spoke and told us, "Do not be afraid. I bring you good news that will cause great joy for all the people. Today in the town of David, a Saviour has been born to you; He is the Messiah, the Lord. This will be a sign you will find a baby wrapped in cloths and lying in a manger."

We just looked at each other, trembling with fear and excitement. We couldn't believe what we were hearing! The angel had just told us that a Saviour, the Messiah has been born in Bethlehem. We have been waiting for the Messiah to come all our lives.

We decided that we would leave the sheep, and go and find the baby! I didn't want to go empty handed, I quickly went over to the sheep, they were all huddled up and I picked up one of my favourite lambs, as I had to take a gift for the Saviour of the World.

We were very humbled and amazed to think that we, just poor shepherds, were the first to hear about the Messiah's birth! Our hearts were full of joy and wonder!

It so happened, that we were in a field just on the outskirts of Bethlehem. We hurried off and found the baby lying in the manger exactly as the angel had said. When we walked into the stable we saw Mary and Joseph and the baby Jesus lying in the manger. There was such a feeling of peace, wonder and joy in the stable that night.

We bowed down in adoration as we looked at Baby Jesus, the Messiah. I laid my lamb down by the manger. The stable was poor and humble but heaven had come down to earth that night!

As we walked out and returned to the fields, we were glorifying and praising God, for all the things we had heard and seen which was exactly as we had been told by the angel.

The Visit Of The Wisemen

We are known as Magi, which means wise men and have come from a country far away in the East. We have astrological and astronomical knowledge, and have studied the stars for many years.

However one day, we saw a very unusual, large and exceptionally bright star in the sky. We had never seen one like it before! It intrigued us as it was so striking and different from other stars we had studied, so we thought it must have royal significance.

We thought about this star long and hard, and we knew that the Christ Child – the Messiah had been born! Nobody had told us we just knew it in our hearts! We had a great desire in our hearts to come and worship him.

There were three of us and we decided to set out on our camels, and follow this unusual beautiful star and see where it took us! We travelled for months and months over deserts, mountain ranges and open plains following the star which kept guiding us!

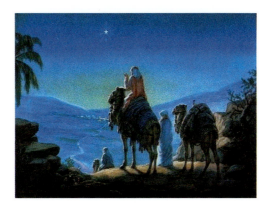

Finally, we arrived in Jerusalem, and at that time Herod was the King. King Herod wanted to meet us, as he had heard about us and wanted to know why we were so interested in the star! We told him that the Christ child had been born in Bethlehem.

King Herod was very worried, and wanted details from us when we saw the star and where exactly this baby was in Bethlehem! King Herod told us to look for the Child, and when we found him, to come back to Jerusalem and let him know, as he was very keen to come and worship the Child too!

We left King Herod, and continued to follow the star which brought us to exactly where Jesus and his Mother Mary were. We were so overjoyed! It had been a long and difficult journey but worth it all!

Immediately, we entered the place where Jesus was, we fell down and worshiped Him, we knew that this was the Messiah, the Saviour of the World! We had been waiting for this moment all of our lives!

We brought him some valuable gifts of gold a precious metal, frankincense which is a perfume or incense, and myrrh which is anointing oil. These precious gifts were typical of what would be presented to a king! We opened them up and gave them to his mother Mary.

The three gifts were chosen for their special symbolism about Jesus himself.

- Gold representing his kingship.
- Frankincense a symbol of his priestly role.
- Myrrh in preparation for his burial and embalming.

THE NATIVITY

After we left Mary and Jesus, we were going to return to King Herod, to tell him all we had seen, but God warned us in a dream that King Herod didn't want to worship Jesus he only wanted to kill Him!

So we decided to go back to our own country by another route.

The Innkeeper gave Jesus, the Saviour of the World a stable where He could be born; the shepherds gave Him a lamb and the Magi, the wise men gave Him Gold, Frankincense and Myrrh.

We can give Him our hearts and our love.

The End

Printed in Great Britain
by Amazon